"One of the best performances of the year."
—*Bob Strauss, Los Angeles Daily News*

"Sarah Silverman, digging so deep into her character that we can feel her nerve endings, is like nothing we've seen before. She's fierce and unerring. No showing off; she just *is*. This is acting of the highest caliber."
—*Peter Travers, Rolling Stone*

"Sarah Silverman's performance should take her career to new places."
—*Alynda Wheat, People*

"Silverman far from anywhere she's been before."
—*Chris Nashawaty, Entertainment Weekly*

"A showcase for Silverman's considerable prowess as a dramatic lead actress. She is completely riveting."
—*Kate Walsh, Indiewire*

"Silverman fills the picture to its very corners. She shows us a person we've never seen before."
—*Stephanie Zacharek, Village Voice*

"Sarah Silverman is an absolute revelation. A tour-de-force, career-changing performance."
—*Scott Mantz, Access Hollywood*

"An amazing and career-changing dramatic turn for Sarah Silverman."
—*Bill Zwecker, Chicago Sun Times*

"Sarah Silverman brings a relentlessly honest and open performance; Oscar worthy in every way."
—*Mark S. Allen, CBS/CW TV*

"Audiences will be wowed by Sarah Silverman's brave, unflinching portrayal."
—*Justine Harman, ELLE.c*

"Powerful. Koppelman's instincts help her navigate these choppy waters with inventiveness and integrity."
—*Los Angeles Times*

"Koppelman mostly writes from inside Laney's disillusioned mind, ricocheting between the quotidian details of wife and motherhood and big-picture musings, forming exquisite stand-alone tone poems."
—*Elle*

"Koppelman's prose style is understated and crackling; each sentence is laden with a foreboding sense of menace. Like a crime scene or a flaming car wreck, it becomes impossible not to stare."
—*Publishers Weekly*

"Koppelman is great at evoking the polarized psychology of a woman pulled between conflicting desires. Imagine the uncompromising sexual prose of the great Tamara Faith Berger merging with an episode of *Mad Men*."
—*Broken Pencil*

"[Koppelman's] brave and challenging look beyond appearances of beauty to the ugly reality of a disturbed mind will remain with readers long after they've finished the book."
—*Library Journal*

"Amy Koppelman probes deeply into the dark and cavernous recesses of a picture-perfect suburban mom, and emerges with one of the most terrifying novels I've read in ages. It's a glorious little explosion of a book."
—*Dani Shapiro*

"Amy Koppleman's *I Smile Back* is a full-throttle, darkly witty, addictive tale of a suburban housewife gone bad, then good, then bad again. What a glittering evil jewel of a character Laney Brooks is!"
—*Jami Attenberg*

I
SMILE
BACK

a novel
AMY KOPPELMAN

Two Dollar Radio
Books too loud to Ignore

TWO DOLLAR RADIO is a family-run outfit founded in 2005 with the mission to reaffirm the cultural and artistic spirit of the publishing industry.

We aim to do this by presenting bold works of literary merit, each book, individually and collectively, providing a sonic progression that we believe to be too loud to ignore.

COLUMBUS, OHIO
For more information visit us here:
TwoDollarRadio.com

BROAD GREEN PICTURES PRESENTS A KOPPELMAN/LEVIEN PRODUCTION IN ASSOCIATION WITH OSCAR CROSBY FILMS AND FILM HOUSE GERMANY AN ADAM SALKY FILM "I SMILE BACK"
SARAH SILVERMAN JOSH CHARLES THOMAS SADOSKI MIA BARRON SKYLAR GAERTNER SHAYNE COLEMAN KRISTIN GRIFFITH WITH CHRIS SARANDON AND TERRY KINNEY
CASTING BY AVY KAUFMAN, CSA EXECUTIVE PRODUCERS SKIP KLINTWORTH JENS MEURER CHRISTIAN ANGERMAYER SUPERVISING SOUND EDITOR ROBERT HEIN MUSIC BY DAVE GOLDEN MUSIC SUPERVISOR ZACK RYAN EDITOR TAMARA MEEM
PRODUCTION DESIGNER BRANDON TONNER-CONNOLLY DIRECTOR OF PHOTOGRAPHY ERIC LIN PRODUCED BY BRIAN KOPPELMAN DAVID LEVIEN MIKE HARROP RICHARD ARLOOK BASED ON THE BOOK BY AMY KOPPELMAN
WRITTEN BY PAIGE DYLAN & AMY KOPPELMAN DIRECTED BY ADAM SALKY

- BROADGREEN -
P I C T U R E S

/ISmileBackMovie   ISmileBackMovie.com   /ISmileBackMovie

I want to thank my agent Andrew Blauner
and my publishers Eric and Eliza Obenauf
for believing in me.

For Brian, Sam, and Anna
and for my mom.

Show me a single wound on earth that love has healed.
　　　　　　　　　　　　　　　—Jim Harrison

I
SMILE
BACK

ACT ONE
North Jersey
Labor Day, 2002

INTERMISSION

ACT TWO
North Jersey
Five weeks later

ACT ONE
North Jersey
Labor Day, 2002

LANEY'S FINGER TRACES HER BREASTS.

Up and around, down. She stops, glances at herself, pushes closer. What Laney sees in the mirror doesn't surprise her anymore. Her body is what it is, ravaged by childbirth, ravaged by too many years of pretending to be naturally thin. People have always told her she's beautiful. People still do, but less than they used to.

Laney starts again, lifting her right breast this time. It is heavier than she thinks it should be, but heavier compared to what? It's hard to remember them before the boob job. It's not like she had perky breasts to begin with. But these? She lets this one fall, and it does, with a nearly inaudible thud, a sound so hollow she wants to crumple up into the shag carpet of her dressing room and disappear.

She looks up and away, then back. There are no new wrinkles. Her mother had wrinkles by this age, but other than the fine lines that flank her mouth, Laney is wrinkle-free. She looks closer. There are, though, two discolorations on her left cheek.

A mole had settled between them, darker than the spots, but not black. She brings the tweezers to her face. Every month or so she finds the mole has sprouted a hair; she plucks the hair. She also grows a hair just under her chin. One dark hair, pubic in texture. She plucks that one too.

Interesting, she thinks, how they grow in a harmony of sorts, the mole hair and chin. They mark the onset of her decline. One day, sooner than later, her kids will flinch when she kisses them. Laney cringes for a second, remembering herself as a little girl, her Aunt Edna's wiry whiskers scraping against her own cheek.

Laney looks closer at her face, then down. Her nipples were deformed. That much she remembers. After the babies they were larger than the silver dollar pancakes the kids eat at IHOP, brown, bumpy. These stand at attention, two bright eyes, ready to eat.

It's not her breasts. Her forehead's smooth, so it's not that either. Is it the liver spots on her face, the mole? Could it be her feet? What's making her feel so ugly?

Laney brings a glass of wine to her mouth, empties it. She checks her feet. No, her feet are okay, a deep plum on her toes. She reminds herself as she rubs the palm of her hand against the bottom of her heel, *soft, still soft*, that she should be happy for this. Some women her age have already lost their feet.

Laney sits, the carpet in her closet, ivory and loose, gathers around her thighs. She puts her still-nice feet out in front of her, stretches her legs, and slides an inch or so back from the mirror. Next to her a jar of rubbing alcohol rests on a lavender hand towel. She opens the jar, dips the tweezers into the liquid, pours herself a second glass of wine.

Laney locates another rogue pube tucked in the crease of her upper thigh. She pushes her thumbs together to loosen it, but the hair won't give. She takes the tweezers, turns its sharp point in the direction of her skin and scrapes. Just a slight sting. She likes to do it this way, dig neatly, draw just a hint of blood before claiming it.

She wipes the hair onto the hand towel, cuts four more times and then stops. She looks back at herself, hating what she sees: her scarred stomach, her fake breasts, the panicked look in her eyes.

Laney leans forward. She never much liked looking at it, not even as a child. She inspects it, all trimmed and waxed. She is more manicured than her front lawn. But it is a used pussy. Stretched out and unforgiving.

Laney pushes herself up off the ground, walks over to the window, and watches her husband practice free throws. Night after night. Bounce. Aim. Shoot. Bruce stops, adjusts the volume on his... do you still call it a boom box? All these years later. Still with "Thunder Road."

She remembers the moment she knew—cruising down the shore, T-tops off, *Born to Run* on the stereo. Buckled, high, wild about fucking on the beach. *Oh my gosh, on the beach, really!?*—this was the man she wanted to spend her life with.

She was silent, timid. Not Bruce. He moaned, keeping time with the waves. He didn't worry about getting busted by some cop. *No one's gonna ruin our good time. I'd never let anyone do that to you, beautiful.*

After, Bruce took her hand and walked her over to that dump of a restaurant that was built to look like a windmill. He ordered cheese fries, a Coke. Laney trailed him up the stairs, sat at the cozy table for two, black resin chairs.

The windmill turned above their heads, cars passed. Laney watched Bruce eat the fries, one after the other, the power in that. She even tasted one, one that he placed on her tongue, thick and hot with cheese. His sweatshirt wrapped around her shoulders. Salty air. Salty fries. She didn't—She simply didn't consider the future.

Laney turns away from the window and walks over to the sink. She opens the medicine cabinet and reaches for a prescription container. She shouldn't but she does.

Her mother once asked Laney how Bruce planned to support them, but Laney ignored her. Choosing instead to fill cardboard boxes with trinkets, giving particular care to a wide and varied collection of colorful glass figurines, while that crazy little dog— the crazy Maltese Bruce gave her for her birthday, ran around her bedroom. *Remember that room you grew up in, who you were back then, when you were a girl still, another girl from a lavender bedroom?*

Laney removes a cotton ball from a covered jar on her vanity, wets it with make-up remover, sweeps it across one eyelid then the other. She rinses, bit by bit, warm sudsy water.

I asked, how are you going to support yourselves?

I'm finishing college, Ma, and Bruce is going to sell insurance.

Please, he's a bookie.

It could be worse. He could be a drug dealer.

Laney kissed her mother on the forehead. She knew how to work her, how to kiss her in such a way that her mother would give her anything—even permission to leave.

You're only twenty-two.

You were nineteen.

And single before thirty.

Ma didn't question after that. Instead, knees firmly planted in carpet, she began folding Laney's winter sweaters.

That dog of yours is going to shit on the carpet.

His name is Jesse James.

Bruce liked those kinds of movies—*Butch Cassidy, Bonnie and Clyde, Josie Wales*—outlaw stuff. Laney liked them too, kind of dangerous, kind of fun.

Fine, Jesse. Jesse James is going to shit on the carpet.

Ma was busy organizing the pile of folded sweaters by color, light to dark, bluish tones to black.

It's August, Ma. It's not like I'm moving across the country. I'll be a half-hour away. I'll come home for these sweaters.

You don't know, she said, *what you need.*

Need?

Laney sinks into warm bath water, slides her neck down cool porcelain. It hadn't occurred to her. What she might need. That she—

It's Labor Day and Laney didn't barbeque. Neighboring beef surrounds them. She stops herself. The sky is clear. A high-pitched whistle is followed by a crackle, then a boom. It used to be that she'd be sad when things ended, but Laney is ready actually, ready for this summer to be over, for the school year to start, for her bad behavior—*Is that what this is?*—to end. Nothing she can't, somehow, reverse has happened, Laney assures herself. She made a few errors in judgment; luckily she got away with them. After her rendezvous with Donny tomorrow, she'll simply stop. Stop with the diversions, no more drinking and drugging. No more fucking around. She will rededicate herself to being a good mom and wife—great mom and wife. There is no need to panic. She hasn't destroyed anything yet.

Tomorrow is the first day of second grade. There will be bake sales again. Everything is okay: her kids are okay—*Remember when I used to light fireworks?*—her husband.

In the fairy-tale there is a knight, a horse, a sunset. In the fairy-tale the princess holds on from behind, her face nestled into her knight's shoulder, the smell of him unmarked as is his character.

An easy clip clopping carries her away from the fortress. *Clip, clop. Clip, clop. Clip, clop.* She, the princess, is wearing a billowing dress, daisies in her hair. She is in white; he is in white, the horse.

Here, in the Garden State, the knight wears Nike t-shirts. Laney sat beside hers, halter-top, capris. She smelled like Fracas, he Paco Rabanne. The engine growled, then jerked as Bruce shifted into drive. He was tan and she was tan. The road stretched out before them, a smooth, even tar and the future simply wasn't something she worried about, not with a new car lease every four years.

Bounce, bounce, swoosh.

Laney adjusts the temperature of the bath water with her toes. Her little girl is fast asleep but her boy, she suspects, her boy who should be sleeping isn't. He's standing by his bedroom window watching his father get the ball in every time. Amazing. He can hear the music his father likes. *Dananana, Dananananananana*. The boy watches in disbelief. Every time.

DananananananaNaNaNaNaNa.

The boy turns from the window, glances at the vintage Knicks poster above his desk: Reed, Monroe, Frazier. On top his desk is a folder, sharpened pencils, and a small box of crayons. On the chair a neatly folded t-shirt, khakis, underwear, socks, clean sneakers. His mother, as usual, has everything organized and ready.

Something isn't right, though. Eli won't be able to explain it, Laney knows. Not tonight. Not ten years from now. The din of it.

What he senses, would put money on if someone offered, is that his mom's crying. No evidence. Just a bouncing ball, Springsteen, and the muffled sound of a lone firecracker. But he'd bet, bet his entire allowance she's crying.

Eli climbs into bed, looks at the poster. They traded Ewing, then Spree. He rolls onto his side, bends his knees, squeezes his eyelids as tight as he can.

Bounce, bounce, swoop.

Laney wishes her boy could see them, the little white lights that are out there tonight, sprinkling themselves across the sky. She wishes, even more, she could show them to him.

LANEY, FRESHLY BATHED, CLOTHED IN

sweats and a tight-fitting tank is sitting, "criss cross applesauce" as her daughter would say, on the bed. A glass of wine in one hand, thumbing through a book with the other. She looks up when Bruce enters, "You know one of these days, honey, you're going to dribble yourself right into a heart attack and there's nothing I can do about it."

Bruce laughs.

Laney smiles.

Look at him: damp jersey, unlaced Jordans, an extra thirty. "Picture it. Me, telling the kids Daddy dropped dead pulling down a rebound."

"Basketball's good exercise." He points to his stomach. "Look at the weight I'm losing, Lane."

Laney brings her knees to her chest, tilts her head slightly to the left. "The treadmill and a little less cream sauce at your business lunches. Do those things, big guy, and you'll be as handsome as Karl Malone in '88."

"Karl Malone is it?" Bruce gestures toward the book, "So what do you think?"

"What do I think about *Insurance and the Meaning of God*, by Bruce Brooks? I think it's brilliant. That whole part about how selling insurance and being a bookmaker are basically the same thing. I love that."

Laney turns to a page she's folded over. "'Selling insurance is no different than bookmaking. Only in this case the insurance company is the house and the house always keeps the vig. Every time you re-up your policy all you're doing is hedging your bet against God.' I mean that's just so great."

"I'm glad you like it." Bruce eases himself onto the mattress, taps his hand against his shorts and motions. Laney, not one to deny, does exactly what he's asking for. She figures any time her husband wants to fuck her she's going to fuck him. Really, how hard is fucking? Not so hard that there aren't a million other girls out there ready, willing, and able to hop on up for a ride.

Still, when they fuck, when she says I love you, when she cooks him his dinner, she's holding back. A dash of salt, a pinch of intimacy. Silly, she knows. Like at this point, with the two kids, not coming is going to protect her somehow, mitigate the inescapable pain.

Laney's been realizing this more and more. How little control she has over things. Say she's persuasive and convinces Bruce to stop playing basketball, then what? He could have a heart attack just as easily on the golf course. Or get into a car accident on the way home from work. Or run off with a waitress.

Laney comes up for air, palms his dick in her right hand to keep it hard, says, "Never mind, okay? Don't quit playing."

Bruce looks at her, the same thrusting, pervasive need in his eyes that got her here in the first place—"Cause I was thinking, there's probably a direct correlation between a guy's retirement from ball and the onset of unfaithful behavior"—that insisted there was still a shot at it for her, some great, warranted, unadulterated chance at happiness.

After, Laney rests her cheek on her pillow, draws a washed-out sea-foam green quilt up past her bare shoulders and closes her eyes. A small lamp is positioned on her bedside table, next to it her wine glass rests on top last week's paperback, a love story.

"Bruce?"

"Yeah, honey?"

"Do you think I'm still a nice person, because I'm not so sure anymore. When I was younger I cared so much about other people. I didn't think I was going to save the world or anything but, you know, I was going to do something meaningful and the truth is, if I died tomorrow I'd have done nothing. No one will remember me."

Bruce rolls over to face her. "You drink too much."

This isn't the conversation she wants to have. "What does drinking have to do with whether or not I'm a nice person?"

Bruce reaches across her body, clicks off the lamp. "Everything, really."

It is dark and there is quiet.

Outside, angry suburban chimneys jab at a nearly perfect evening sky. Somewhere perhaps, a song is playing; a cruiser from their time, one of those great mix-tape, roll-down-your-window, cigarette-smoking tunes.

Bruce kisses the back of his wife's head, "You're the nicest girl in the world, Lane. That's why I married you."

A GUARD, A GUY SHE'S NEVER SEEN

before, is standing at the school's entrance directing traffic. Laney fixes her hair, checks her teeth for lipstick, lowers her window.

"Only school busses allowed through here," he says pointing in the direction of the elementary school lot.

Laney takes a second, leans forward. "But I've been double parking and running my son in for…"

"Ma?" Eli says nervously.

Laney turns around—"Don't worry, honey"—turns back, "Is Frank here? He always lets me double park."

"Frank's guarding the door." New Guy points to the sheet of paper in his other hand, "It's all here."

Not completely indifferent to the sight of Laney, her hair blown straight, mascara, lip-gloss, he folds the memo in half, bends it this way and that. "Makes for a good paper plane," he says as it wafts into the car.

The funny guy at the office, Laney thinks.

"Ma?"

"Give me a second, hon." Laney puts up her window.

As if one pockmarked security guard is going to ward off a terrorist insurgence. Laney unfolds the plane.

Dear Families,
 Regrettably, the tragic events of last year brought the issue of school security to our attention. As a precaution,

no vehicles, other than school busses, will be allowed to park in front of school…

The eloquence of the PTA. Such foresight. Better make sure those moms with the truckloads of explosives aren't allowed within twenty feet of the place. This, yet another false sense of security perpetuated by women who think—actually believe—their husbands will still want to fuck them as long as they put in the hours on the treadmill. Oh—the joys of drop off.

"What does it say, Ma?"

Laney puts the car in reverse. "Says we have to park in the lot."

And now an early morning squeeze between a sister Denali and a Suburban of all things.

The more kids you have the larger the truck?

Too bad the equation doesn't work like that. The Suburban, with seats for nine belongs to, "Hey, Diane." Laney waves her over. "Can I fit?"

Diane walks round, motions with her hands, "A little more to the left…"

Let's see: Diane has one kid. A son, plus a husband, a dog, and sometimes a babysitter equals five empty passenger seats. Laney has two kids, and a husband, and occasionally her mother comes to visit. It's a tie, ladies and gentleman. Both of these women are guilty of profligate behavior. "Turn. Great, now straighten out your wheel."

Laney should have known better than to fall for the easy con. A sports utility vehicle? She realigns her wheels, glides into the spot with relative ease. Good thing they put power steering in these off-roaders. Jersey shore in the summer. The Caribbean for winter vacation. As if they were going to find time to hit a campground?

There's the safety argument, but honestly, the whole SUV thing's a rite of passage more than anything else. Not much different from her engagement ring: Laney fell in love, Bruce gave her a ring, they married.

A little into it they fucked for a kid. Squeezed one out. Couple years later fucked for another. Now she's here. One more broad in a big-ass truck with the ring, the two kids, the latest cell phone.

Laney hops out, opens the door for Eli. "I can't believe this. I think I forgot the Parent ID they sent us in the mail." Laney feels the familiar edge coming on, she has to calm down, if she forgot the pass she forgot the pass. It's not like they don't know her here. She checks her pockets, sifts through her bag.

Hearing the panic in Laney's voice, Diane says, "What are you driving yourself crazy for? I'll vouch for you."

See what a nice place this is to raise a family? Everything is pretty and safe. The people are nice. This is why Bruce mortgaged them to the hilt.

Cause it's an easy life?

Sure, is there something wrong with wanting an easy life? No stabbings at the town deli. No homeless people waiting at the market with outstretched arms and paper cups to remind you that—

People are hungry?

"ID?"

"I forgot it today," Laney says to Sally Frasier, the lower school principal.

"Parent IDs are mandatory this year."

"I'll vouch for her," Diane says with a smile. A comrade in this act of mothering: lights, camera, action.

The lower school principal shakes her head.

"Ma?" Eli looks to his mother for assurance.

"Sally, I've been coming here for two years. It's the first day of school. Can't you make an exception?"

"If I make an exception for you I'll have to make one for everyone. Eli's familiar with Mrs. Nero. He spent time in her class at the end of last year."

This, Laney knows, is about more than a flimsy paper ID.

This is Sally's way of evening the playing field. Laney might live in a nicer house, have two children and a husband who loves her but for eight hours a day, Sally reigns. Throughout this duration both Eli and his mother must abide by her rules. And you can bet your diamond studs Sally Frasier would never forget her ID.

Laney's tired of it, of being judged by disapproving women. All of them sure they'd never be like her. Never get tripped up by a car salesman. Never forget their ID.

Sure, Laney's perfected the whole down-to-earth, I-don't-give-a-shit thing. But beneath the deliberate surface, black t-shirt, jeans, Sally Frasier knows the truth. Laney's no different than a whore.

This morning she woke, showered, dressed, and ran to the kitchen. She threw eggs in a pan, a smile on her face. "Good morning," she said as they entered.

She wasn't being insincere. She was happy, genuinely, to see her boy and girl, her husband. She wanted them to have a healthy start to their day. Nevertheless breakfast isn't an option. It's what she gets paid for: French toast, freshly squeezed orange juice, enough maple syrup in the pantry to keep a family of four going twenty years.

"I'm okay, Ma."

Laney is almost too ashamed to look at him, "You sure?"

Eli takes a deep breath, secures his knapsack on his shoulders, "I'm sure."

Powerless to the authorities that be, Laney releases him. There he goes, down a crowded hall, one foot followed by another.

Just outside the classroom he stops, turns, looks to his mother. He waits, doesn't move, for the kiss she's blown to reach him. He tucks it in his pocket, then walks through the classroom door. Safe and sound. Sheltered within the confines of a set curriculum.

LANEY IS SURE THAT THE SPOTS ON

her cheek are laughing at her for believing she could follow through with this. Another year of elementary school: boring play dates, empty conversations, all in pursuit of some vague image of motherly love. Laney brakes for some broad making a right into the tennis center, pops open the glove compartment, grabs an Ultra Light. That's a choice, Laney thinks as she lights the cigarette. Drop your kid off at school, smack a few buckets of balls with a cute pro.

Laney glances at herself in the rearview mirror. She knows what she's going to do. She's going to get the number of a dermatologist from her mother, have the spots erased. Laney reaches for her cell phone, scrolls down. When she sees his text she smiles.

DONNY: You'd kiss me if I was Buck Dharma.

LANEY: You don't have a mustache.

DONNY: Fu Manchu, Pancho Villa, you name it.

She looks at the large gray cooler on the passenger seat. Fuck the 9/11 widows who think they own the market on grief. Laney hates herself for thinking this, who's she to determine the length of mourning? Still, it's coming up on the anniversary and what happened that day is like anything else now. All those bodies falling through the sky subsist in collective memory.

Manipulated images as disconnected as any other memory. Even more so. Because, let's be real for a second. Laney didn't know anyone who died. Hers is a misappropriated sorrow.

Laney atones with care packages. The organization she belongs to, the only organization she belongs to, The Dinner Angels, delivers food to the victims' families. The assignments, which rotate, are sent by email. Head count, specified preferences, notation of food allergies. But nothing personal. No names. No stories.

At first Laney was bothered by the formality. But it's probably smart, keeps the whole thing at arm's length, no obligation other than food.

To compensate for the disconnect, Laney works extra hard on what she refers to as her "widow menu." Preparing dishes that can linger a few days. Always with a protein: Chicken Gumbo, Beef Bourguignon, Tuna Loaf. Today she went for simple Meat Lasagna. A salad, some fruit. She baked a batch of cookies, threw in a small bag of gumballs. But it is, there's no denying, getting silly already.

She pulls up to an unassuming row house. Fireman? Police? Bond Broker? Mom? Who is it? Who is missing from this house? Laney places the cooler on the front stoop, next to a child's rake and a pair of muddy sneakers. And yet to love. To keep on loving.

Her phone beeps again.

DONNY: You coming?

LANEY: Why do you love me so much?

DONNY: Because you're beautiful, funny, smart.

The smart part makes Laney laugh.

LANEY: What about Sheryl?

DONNY: Sheryl loves you too.

LANEY: I'm being serious.

DONNY: I told you, I'll leave Sheryl.

Laney heads to the city. Pays toll. Enters. Throughout the

darkened tunnel, lights blink. One after the next, their message dubious. On the far side, Laney will evade this self. There, straddling finely threaded sheets, she is other, her face pressed up against a leather headboard evoking. She's done this before. Many times.

Laney met Jack Sigerson, an English banker, in the bar at the Regency. He insisted, for quite some time, nearly an hour, on retaining the jacket of his tweed suit. She gripped his tie; capable he was of all sorts of pleasures. And she too, bestowed. Her long legs a bridge to the part of him unfed. Her breasts—a silver tray could balance—a glass of wine, his blood pressure medicine.

Immersed, in the absence of fear the predator's nose sprang forth anointing itself conqueror. It made her laugh, his toothy grin. To be master over what cannot love. Blissfully unaware that it was she who gave the order to release. Hers a long, extended moan.

The affair ended after his third visit and not because Laney was caught or because she felt particularly guilty, for that matter. The affair with Jack came to an end because like with everyone else, except Cowboy, when she fucked Jack she felt nothing.

Cowboy, her first, fucked liked he tasted. Warm, dusty, almost new. With him Laney was able to focus. Ignore the rain outside. Better yet, turn it into a storm from an airport bodice ripper—thick, thundering, cooling down the heat of their passion. But that was last spring at a dude ranch in Wyoming.

Today's sojourn isn't about escape. Today is about carelessness. There are rules: not tempting your friend's husband is one of them. But Laney has a plan. She'll fuck Donny just once, just enough to demystify herself, just enough to get him to go away.

Laney parks her car in a garage and heads north up Madison. It's a gorgeous day and she's thankful for the bright sun, cooler air. Weather, she thinks, is impartial. You don't need to be principled to enjoy a breezy day like this. You merely have to be alive.

She stops in front of a jewelry store window. Handsome diamond rings stand erect in their case, pledging a radiant future. Laney smiles at the sight of a modest cushion cut. They are, she thinks, really pretty diamonds.

Laney's taking her time. Anticipation is a potent aphrodisiac. She glances into a bakery. Look at those adorable cookies. She enters, waits her turn, "I'd like…" She buys two: a baseball shape for Eli, a pumpkin for Janey. She exits, moves forward, fingering the two colorful cookies in her pocketbook. On the street two nannies, each with a stroller, approach then pass. Behind them, a blonde woman is pushing a wheelchair. A man is belted to the chair. A legless man in a yellow oxford.

Laney doesn't know quite what to do because she doesn't have sunglasses on and it's impolite to stare. So she smiles what she hopes is an I'm-not-scared-to-look-at-you smile. The pair acknowledge her smile with a nod. Laney's well practiced, communicating she's sorry without pity.

Laney pictures the legless man at home. He is out of his wheelchair, propped up on the floor of his den, same yellow oxford. Supported, his back against the base of a tan leather couch, the edge of a wooden coffee table pressing gently up against his stomach.

She imagines him content, spooning, with these giant hands of his, Breyer's vanilla bean into his mouth. He has a kid next to him, also with the ice cream. They are watching a baseball game. Kid's eight years old, Yankee fan.

The attractive blonde who was pushing him earlier is sitting on the couch, her legs brush against the side of his head. The boy, and the blonde woman, the legless man's son and wife, stand at commercial. The boy bends over, gives his father a kiss goodnight and walks out the room with his mother.

The man remains, switching the channels back and forth.

"Survivor," CNBC, "SportsCenter." He wants more ice cream, pushes the palms of his hands against the floor. But there's no way, no way he has the strength to boost himself back up into his wheelchair. He calls out, calls his wife's name but she doesn't hear him or she hears him but doesn't answer because she's upstairs busy putting their boy to bed. It's been a long day, hasn't she done enough?

Some time passes, nearly an inning, the boy must be fast asleep by now. He looks in the direction of the phone. The light's on but he can't reach the receiver. He wouldn't interrupt anyway.

Whatever she's doing with whomever it is she's speaking to mitigates some of the guilt. What's she going to do, live out the rest of her life never getting laid? She didn't sign up for this.

But our legless man wants a little more ice cream; it tastes sweet, feels smooth, goes down easy.

Growing up, his dad had a small lighting shop down in the Bowery. Guy worked like a dog, six, seven days a week. Back then they didn't have Little League per se, but there were weekly games in the neighborhood. Usually Sunday afternoons; his dad could have been up all night stocking light bulbs, never missed a game.

And after the game, win or lose, the legless man, not yet legless, and his father would stop at the luncheonette on the corner. He'd get a double scoop of vanilla, his father a malted. They'd sit at the counter, talk about Mantle, Ruth, walk home hand in hand.

Those were probably his happiest times. Hard pressed to find anything that duplicates the feeling of smacking a ball and running to first. Especially now. He looks up at the phone, then down to where his legs used to be, then forward at the game. Godammit, couldn't she put that guy on hold, run him over a scoop, and pick back up again?

His wife tries her best, really she does, but she just doesn't get it. No one really gets it. Although he's pretty certain a guy who's lost his sight would. You walk a blind guy into the middle of the Yankee outfield, sit him down, give him a piece of grass to chew—miraculously the guy'd see green—limegreen, yellowgreen, every kind of fucking green you can imagine.

Our guy cocks his head, raises the bowl to his mouth, licks the last bit of flavor off the bottom. Just another night for him, another green field fading to black.

Laney is thinking about this as Donny fucks her. It feels good getting fucked in the ass like this. The pain, a final and utter submission. No man, she thinks, can love a girl whose ass he fucked.

Or even think he loves.

Later, on her back, a red lollipop in her mouth, Laney's mind drifts. If the guy just had legs, even legs that didn't work, Laney would feel better. Maybe with technology, a computer chip linked to something in the brain, maybe one day he walks right on out of that chair, takes his boy to practice, stopping for a cone on the way home. Stumps, not much you can do with those. Only the complete absence of hope can render a pain this abbreviated and concise. Funny, she thinks, how the appearance of normalcy is secondary to reality. She says this out loud but Donny's fast asleep.

At rest he looks like his son, mouth open, at peace. She can keep it going, let him buy her stuff. A bag from Bottega, a watch from Cartier. All Laney'd have to do is ask and Donny would happily pay the balance on her Bergdorf charge. He would. He'd do that and more, all the while promising to love her without conditions. But in the end he'll want more. Every man wants more.

And that's the funny thing, Laney thinks as she pulls up her panties. I can love you and you can love me and still it can mean nothing. Nine years of marriage, two kids, three thousand marinated chicken breasts—and nothing.

Funnier still—Laney grabs what's left of the eightball off the coffee table, rummages through Donny's jacket, finds his wallet, grabs forty bucks for parking, and exits the rented suite. In, then out, then in again—How we'll do almost anything to keep it that way.

Later, about twenty minutes, Donny will wake to an empty bed. He will check his watch for the time, his cell for missed calls. He'll stretch his arms up over his head and perhaps grin. Following this abbreviated period of revelry he will push himself up and out of bed. It's time to go home.

But, first a shower.

Donny will open the door to the bathroom, grab a towel, fumble before finding the light. But even in the dark there's no mistaking. Scribbled on the mirror, red lipstick an effective cliché, he reads the words out loud:

"Don't leave Sheryl."

A moment will pass but only a moment.

Then Donny will turn on the faucet, wait for the water to steam, and enter.

LANEY HAS TWO THOUGHTS ON HER

mind as she drives home. Two non sequiturs. Disjointed and unrelated.

One: If a person were to dive into a pool and shout from under water would a guest at the barbeque hear him?

Two: If a person were to light a firecracker in an illuminated sky would it shine?

The answers, she reminds herself, don't matter. Because what she really wants to know is this: If a woman fucks her girlfriend's husband does she deserve to live?

Laney sees, but can't hear, the traffic racing along Highland Avenue. Hungry, broken people chasing after things. She grips the steering wheel. *Not me.* Places her foot on the gas. *No more wanting.*

She must hurry, must do this before she's overcome by doubt. No, that's not it, not exactly. She isn't doubtful. This is the right thing to do, the only thing. Still, she feels bad. Because it isn't like she doesn't know—she knows—how much this will hurt them.

But Laney is now, simply, too tired to fight. All these years of insisting this is what she wants out of life.

Drive me, fuck me, feed me.

For what?

So Eli can use Phish lyrics against her, "You're wrong, Ma.

'Farmhouse' is not about hope." A fourteen-year-old Janey hovering, black nail polish, vintage Cobain t-shirt. It's only a matter of time until Laney is marked irrelevant by her children. They'll continue to love her, that's what kids do. But their love will stem from obligation. A sense of duty. Guilt.

The earlier they learn to hate me the better.

She's certainly left enough clues—drugs, adultery, suicide—for them to know that it wasn't their fault. Their mother was simply a fucked-up human being, damaged. Which will be disturbing in its own way, but at least her kids won't be confused. At least they won't think they could have saved her. Contempt, Laney rationalizes, will be their salvation. If her history has taught her anything it's that hate, not love, is the more powerful of the two emotions.

Anyway, there's no retro-alternative, no going back and fixing things. Of course she can continue doing the expected, pick Eli up from school, bring him home, continue to pretend. But really, what's that going to do for him? It's only a matter of time until he figures out the truth, until he sees how ugly his mother really is.

No. What is, was, could be, doesn't matter—Laney stops herself. She signals her blinker, turns. Home is a construct. Laney is at peace with her decision. Mostly because she finally gets it. She can keep fucking around. She can fuck every guy with two balls and a cock and it won't matter. There's nothing left to reclaim. Home doesn't apply to her anymore.

Laney hears herself laughing, the same wicked, taunting little laugh of this afternoon. It is the sound of resignation. Utter and indistinguishable.

Obscured by a film of tears it takes Laney a moment to locate herself. There she is, hidden in the soft sheets of childhood. She, his only, tucked under a sea-foam green blanket, a ballerina nightgown, a stuffed bear.

Her father taps her shoulder, "Honey?"

It is night, the bedroom dark, she focuses—there's Dad, "Daddy?"

"I need you to listen to me. I want to make sure you understand what I was saying to your brother tonight. Never chase after a hat, you understand?"

Laney nods her head.

"It's just not worth it. Some things, no matter how hard—"

Laney remembers her father leaning over to kiss her, one soft kiss on her left cheek. Then standing and walking out the door. Another guy just shy of a real six feet tall.

In spite of the clarity of this memory, or maybe because of it, Laney's not certain if this actually happened. It could be a recollection that she, as a child, pieced together. A line from a movie, a scene in a book.

Did her father come into her room the night he left? Did he say good-bye or simply walk out the door? Did his breath smell like single malt, or lo mein? Does it even matter?

Truth is secondary to belief. However it took form, a message was imparted. The Yankee cap Mike Kalinsky stole from her brother earlier that day symbolized hope. Dad didn't want either of them chasing after it. To hope is futile when the only absolute is death. Laney lets out a long exhausted breath. She's not scared or even sad. Having neither the energy nor desire to burrow through the grief she surrenders.

"I promise, Daddy." The echo of this final untainted conviction gives her strength.

The FedEx truck she's been stuck behind turns left into Town Plaza. The road before her is open now, dotted by a few passing cars, a navy Volvo wagon, a Mercedes sedan. The traffic light at the intersection up ahead is changing from green to yellow to—Laney closes her eyes, presses her foot deeper into the gas, hands up, letting go.

AT THE OUTSKIRTS OF HAPPINESS A

girl dances. Arms open, she floats. Eager and unafraid. Birds fly by overhead inviting her to join them. Separate yes, but together they are happy. Warm.

Fragments of pussy willows drift along with the wind that carries them and she remembers how she loved him. No guilt. No pandering. The way he tucked her hair behind her ears, his half-smile, hers.

She forgets, what it was he said as he looked at her, what promises were made, then revoked. This, the artificial versus the real. This, the fine line that divides hate from love, you from me.

In a cinnamon-scented home a candle burns for the idle lonely. They are other.

Created, God's children, in his image. Yet we insist on melding ours to our own. The dilution of spirit as accidental as an ill-chosen toenail polish.

The dishwasher clangs, the fridge belches as Laney scrubs a non-stick pan. Somewhere in time, both then and now, she shines. Naked beneath a roof of content, a gleaming stove reflects her beauty. Even so, she hates.

Laney bends over, settles the plate of cookies before her children, warm, pure. No hydrogenated oils. No preservatives. They will rot if not consumed. Sooner rather than later.

Lane, you see my cell?

She locates her husband's phone between cushions of the couch, hands it to him.

You're the greatest.

Remembrance. Cookies and milk. A misplaced cell phone. The smell of a white colt named Frances.

You want to go for a ride?

These moments followed by a slow and significant fade to black.

Peace. Peace at any price. What price peace?

A melody of screeching brakes and bellowing horns inform this scene. One more startled chorus quieted by the still voice of the resolute.

You know what happens when you feed the birds? They forget to fly south and freeze to death.

Laney's eyes jerk open.

She is safe. On the far side of the intersection, untouched.

Laney takes a deep breath, pulls over to the side of the road. One by one the beleaguered cars pass. There is an eye roll from a lady in a silver Jag. A Mexican, standing in the back of a gardening truck flips her the bird. But that's about it. No one bothers to stop, ask if she is okay. But if someone were, to stop, would she even want them to?

Laney presses her forehead against the steering wheel. She should call Donny, after what she gave him today he'd be more than happy to come get her, take her for a drink, calm her down.

Nah, she's had enough of Donny, his empty heroics, his grin. Bruce. She'll call Bruce, call her husband. She dials.

"Bruce Brooks' office."

"Hi, Jules, Bruce there?"

"Sorry, Mrs. Brooks, Mr. Brooks has a meeting outside the office. Why don't you try him on his cell?"

Laney presses the digits but doesn't send. What's she going to say: Bruce, honey, I was in the city fucking Donny and I felt so guilty about it that I ran a red at the Town Plaza intersection. I thought maybe I'd be lucky and—

And what? Die? Is that it, Laney? You want to die?

Rhetoric. His questions. Her answers.

As if what she wants can be determined in a course of minutes on a cellular phone. His single deep breath would infuriate her.

She glances at the Pathmark sign down the road. Two percent? Skim? There are options. She could buy groceries.

Even better she could just stop doing this, "acting out" as her mother calls it. Laney glances at the dash, 2:15. Shit. She's running out of time. If she plans on picking Eli up from school she better get going.

Laney switches to FM, plays with the dial.

I wish I was a sailor man with someone who waited for me...

Dips her free pinky into the recently pilfered baggie of cocaine—

I wish I was as fortunate, as fortunate as me...

Breathes in—

I wish I was a messenger and all the news was good...

Releases the sunroof—

I wish I was the full moon shining off your Camaro's hood...

Vedder, Laney brings a cigarette to her lips, presses the lighter, waits for it to pop, "*I wish I was the verb 'to truth' that never let you down.*"

Tears trickle down the sides of her face, she grins, inhales, shifts gears.

"Fucking, Eddie Vedder."

VISINE: TWO DROPS IN EACH EYE. A

squirt of Afrin up both nostrils. Laney rummages through her concealment bag, an unassuming turquoise satchel. Blush. Lipstick. Powder. All this so that when Carly's mom asks her if she's okay, "You okay, Lane?"

Laney can answer, "Of course." Confident her eyes are clear she's able to push the sunglasses up on her head—as if to prove it—as if to say, "Look at my eyes, don't I look okay?"

But she's not okay, now is she? After all, Sheryl's walking toward her. What if she smells him on—"Hey, Sher," Laney says. A quick kiss hello.

"Where do you want to go to dinner Saturday?" Sheryl asks.

Laney shrugs her shoulders. "You guys pick."

"Italian, Chinese?" and so the conversation continues. Two friends making dinner plans for Saturday night.

Thankfully, there is much territory to cover before dismissal: afterschool activities to sign up for, play dates to be arranged, fundraisers to organize. "Sure," Laney hears herself answering, another bright red lollipop in her mouth, "I'd be happy to help with the coat drive."

The clock ticks, time passes, and the mothers, which she is considered one of, cluster about. A swarm of bees sucking pollen from flower, life from child. Unaware, most, that assassin bugs often hide in the flower's core.

The buzzer rings. Laney: bee, flower, assassin, stands at attention. Somehow she persists. In spite of—is that right? Or because of? Because he didn't? Does it matter? He left then. She's here now.

When Eli sees her, he nearly runs but stops himself. He proceeds, one foot in front of the other, a large sheet of oak-tag trailing behind him.

The knee is the first thing she comments on, "What happened to your knee, E?"

"I fell."

"You fell?"

"Miss Aboitiz cleaned it, put a Band-Aid on it."

She looks at him then. This boy, her life.

"Miss Aboitiz says there's nothing a Band-Aid can't fix."

Yet again, Laney is reminded of the inanity of this choice. To live, to continue in this fashion. A modern day Wonder Woman: jeans, sandals, a lousy Band-Aid from the school nurse.

"What's that you got there?"

"Nothing."

"Come on, E. Let me see what you did at school today."

Eli hands it over.

"Great teepee. I loved learning about the Indians."

"Native Americans, Ma."

"I'm sorry, honey." Laney runs her fingers through Eli's thick hair.

"Do you know that the Pilgrims stole America from the Native Americans? They had the Native Americans teach them how to fend through winter, grow corn and stuff and then stole their land."

"Really?"

"So we gave them casinos."

"Who said that?"

"Nicky. His mom told him."

Laney pictures Nicky's do-gooder mom, her large white home, her checkbook.

"Nicky says Thanksgiving's a lie."

Laney wants to say, "Yeah, honey, shit happens. Shit happens and there's nothing you can do about it." She wants to tell him that Nicky's mom is right. The Pilgrims lied.

But it's more complicated than that. It's not like they were sitting there on the *Niña, Pinta, Santa María* thinking: I can't wait to get to whatever it was they called America back then and exploit the red man. Desperation, not desire, is the root of atrocity.

And fear.

"No more dilly-dallying. Your sister's been waiting all day for us." Laney helps her son with his seatbelt, draws the sunshade, and hops into the front seat. She'll drive home, cook dinner. The kids will eat, take baths, wait for Daddy.

Laney needs cigarettes and lollipops.

"Hey, E," she says as they pull up to 7-Eleven. "Let's have a cold cereal party."

Eli smiles, looks up at her. "Really?!"

"Any cold cereal you want."

Laney and her son move through the aisle, "Lucky Charms. Got it."

She takes note of his forgiving voice, nodding her head every so often.

His sentences are short. Simple words, name brands that conjure familiar smells, "Got the Frosted Flakes in my hand." Safety.

If one were to look closely, like the man behind the cash register does, he might notice the tears beginning to pool in Laney's eyes. "Of course you can get Cap'n Crunch." A breath. "It isn't a cold cereal party without Crunch Berries."

There is, Laney thinks to herself as she walks out of the

market, a thing called happiness. Hers is no longer the blameless happiness she dreamed of. Happiness, real happiness must be accounted for.

There, in the middle of Town Plaza, the cool autumn air pressing against her cheeks, she looks up at the blue sky and then straight ahead toward home. She's not quite sure whom to thank, Tony the Tiger, the checkout guy, God? In truth it doesn't matter. Belief itself lends hope.

Laney drives. She passes the same tall trees, turns at the same corner, stops at the same stop sign she has passed, turned, stopped at for these last six years. It would be great if she could say that the life she's living here in Jersey is a big surprise to her. That she came from a small town in the Midwest, grew up milking cows and didn't know any better. That she's an innocent, or even something close to that.

But she's not.

In truth, there's nothing inconsistent with what Laney wanted and what she got for herself. She grew up in the city, thought the suburbs might be different and they are. But not that different. Both are a variation on the same theme. The act of striving, the disappointment, regret. People in the city just wear better costumes.

Laney had the Naf Naf sweatshirts, the Tiffany Bangles. But back then she played a minor role, the pretty daughter in the pretty apartment. Here in Short Hills she's a main player, so it's different to a certain extent.

Still, she can't say that she didn't have full understanding of how the story, her story, would lay itself out way before she raced down that aisle. But this was her chance godammit. She was going to show the world how it should be done.

Laney wasn't going to draw the blinds, take a Valium, crawl into bed like her mother did. She certainly wasn't going to let her husband walk out the door one afternoon—

She stops herself. It's funny, how everything changes and

somehow nothing changes. Sometimes, when she gets down, she thinks maybe that's just the way it is.

Janey's waiting at the front door with the sitter, same knobby knees, same kinky hair Laney had as a child. As Laney waves to her daughter it becomes clear. She must protect her kids, not allow them to compromise, to break, to become anything like her.

If it takes her the rest of her life she will teach both her children to simply accept. There are people like that, people who don't beat themselves up, don't take every little injustice personally. Those people, same callous fuckers that walk past a legless guy without pause, those are the ones who win.

The little girl opens the door, "MOMMY!"

She likes me. She really likes me.

Frankly, at the end, Laney won't be thinking of Bruce, or Eli for that matter, but of Janey's arms. As they are now. Wrapped tightly around her mother's neck. The little girl clings.

Laney pretends this doesn't frighten her. She'll be here long enough. To see Janey marry? Have a baby? When would be a safe time for Laney to close her eyes, fade to black?

Now, icing a cake, chocolate with vanilla butter-cream. Janey gets upset, "It's not the way I pictured it." She gestures for her mother to wipe her face, then flinches when Laney comes at her with a napkin. "It's not perfect."

"Nothing's perfect" is Laney's response. She should say, "Janey, honey, things don't need to be perfect." This is, after all, one cake. Singular. "We can bake another one tomorrow." She could convey this but doesn't.

Instead, Laney, anxious that she might snap—comedown is always a bitch—walks over to the fridge and pours herself a tall glass of orange juice. "Go watch a little TV with your brother. I have to finish getting dinner ready."

Well aware that the preparation of her weeknight screwdriver should remain a covert operation, Laney waits until the little girl is all the way down the hall before adding vodka. This is what Laney does when she scares herself. She relies on the television and Absolut.

Bruce pulls into the driveway, shifts gears, shuts the engine. He walks toward the house, one of thousands: suit, tie, loafers. Laney opens the door for him.

"Smells delicious," Bruce says, a quick kiss on the lips. "What's for dinner?"

"Roast chicken, broccoli—"

Bruce sorts through the mail, "Sounds good."

"And watermelon."

"Great, honey. Hey, where are the kids?"

"In the den watching television."

Bruce gives Laney another quick kiss, "I'll go let them know I'm home."

And then, just as Laney begins to set the table she hears it. "Daddy!" This, the sound of her children cheering upon their father's return, marks the passing of another day. Laney takes a long, deep breath. I've gotten away with it again, she thinks, then wonders, silverware in hand, what or which thing exactly she's gotten away with.

LATER, AFTER DINNER, KNOWING THE

chorus—sampled—Laney sings along. Impressed, Eli, that his mother knows the words—"I used to listen to The Police all the time when I was around your age"—the son watches his mother sway. There are several ways Eli can relate this moment. For Laney there is only this: she misses him. Already. But then she missed him before he was even born.

Hope dashes. Clichés ring true. Frozen turkey is on sale at C-town. Time passes faster and more slowly than you want it to. If only Laney could deposit these moments. Withdraw them later. When she is too tired to remember. Or can't. And now?

Now it's bathtime.

Laney passes Eli the soap. "Honey," she says with a smile, "what's the point if you don't use soap?" Eli, eager to catch the outcome of the Yankee game, grins his newly toothless grin, shrugs his shoulders, and hurries through his washing.

Laney is fine with this. She waits, her drink on top the toilet bowl, Janey by her side, for Eli to signal. As soon as he does she opens her arms. He huddles between them, nice warm towel. "Ma," he says, trying to escape.

What to do?

No need to fret. Laney opens her arms. She needs to work harder on this managing her fears. So Eli goes. Scurrying down the hall.

Faster than a speeding bullet.

A white terry cape draped around his shoulders.

More powerful than a locomotive.

Laney follows him into his bedroom. Janey trails behind.

Able to leap tall buildings in a single bound.

The whole thing is kind of nice.

It's a bird. It's a plane.

Laney blinks and Eli is a little boy in costume.

It's Superman.

She blinks back.

Her son, her naked son, has positioned himself right in front of the television screen. Laney stands at the edge of his doorway, takes in his broadening frame. His shoulders, his back. She nods. A tribute to the life-size Jeter poster across from Eli's bed. *Smug motherfucker.*

Laney doesn't need any more reminders. She knows she should let it go, let Eli dry off in the air-conditioning. What's the worst that can happen? Eli doesn't towel off properly and catches a chill?

She is being ridiculous. Eli isn't going to catch a chill and even if he does, so what? It's a Yankee game, a close Yankee game and—

"E," Laney says. No response. "Eli!"

He turns. There she is, his mother. At the door, hair bunched in a pony.

One hand on hip, the other dangling a t-shirt. Laney is aware that this could be the moment he'll choose to remember. On a date with some cute first-year psyche major.

What's your mom like?

My mom?

Still, Laney can't help herself. "I need you to put on this t-shirt," she says.

The command unwavering, steadfast, the Amazon warrior.

Eli throws it over his head and turns back to the game. Laney kneels, lifts his towel off his carpet and tosses it to him, "And dry those balls of yours."

That gets him. He turns, looks at her with a studied coldness, then as if to underscore he rolls his eyes.

"Really. I don't want you to get a rash."

Laney tries at least not to be foreboding. Her delivery is lighthearted. Isn't Eli laughing? Janey? Aren't they all laughing?

"BRUCE?"

"Yeah, babe."

Bruce is standing over the toilet bowl clipping his toenails. He has a Q-tip balanced in each ear as if to call attention to the entirely superfluous secretion.

Laney watches him through the open bathroom door. She should ask him. After all, how's she supposed to know? He's the guy.

"What, honey?"

Bruce turns, his towel wrapped around his waist like a good boy.

"I was just wondering, what you do about your balls."

"What?"

Laney's not sure if her husband didn't hear her cause he's busy excavating earwax or if he simply didn't understand her question. So she asks again, more clearly this time, "After a shower do you worry about drying your balls?"

"Do I *worry*?"

"Like when you were a little boy, did your mother teach you to dry your balls or did you just know to do it, like instinctively?"

Bruce stops with the Q-tip, checks to see what he collected, then looks at her.

"How many drinks does that make?"

Laney looks at her glass, "Obviously not enough."

Bruce shakes his head, "You dry them like any other part of your body."

"Oh."

Laney waits until he finishes with his other ear, "And what happens if you don't dry them? Do you get a rash?" She can see he's thinking. Pitiful, the effect she has on people.

"I guess you could, but mostly I think whatever you don't get just dries in your underwear."

Your underwear!

Laney wants to jump out of bed, swear to God. She wants to jump out of bed, run down the hall, barrel into her son's room.

You have nothing to fear, Eli. You have underwear!

Laney nearly giggles from the poetry of it.

"Hm," Bruce says, bending over her. It's reasonable though, him mistaking her interest in balls for interest in his balls. She goes along with it, easy enough. Amazing, she thinks as they do it. All that worrying and underwear. God damn.

In the midst of this performance her dad enters. Not in a dirty way. He's fully dressed, black jeans, a t-shirt. Nothing sexual. He simply appears, plopping himself on the chintz loveseat across the foot of her bed. He sits there, pressing his index finger to the tip of his nose, motioning Laney to keep quiet. *Fuck, you're beautiful.* And then he winks. It's the craziest thing, his wink. How it reassures her.

"Uh," Bruce jabs it in. "Uh," again. Two more thrusts and he's relieved himself. Laney waits a minute before standing, then stands. She makes her way toward the bathroom shaking her head as she goes. Giddy. She can't help herself, smiling as she is. Tighty-whities and a Band-Aid from the school nurse. How fantastic.

The last, and only time, was for drinks. Dad wanted to congratulate her, to know about her, about Bruce. They met at a bar. Sometime between Thanksgiving and Christmas, little white lights twinkled from artificial trees. He gave her a comfortable hug, as if it had been days, not years. "My gosh," he said as they sat, "My gosh."

There was some small talk. He enjoyed Florida, the warm weather, the easy lifestyle.

Mom?

Mom was doing well. Dating a nice man.

Your brother?

Rooster was great too, loves LA, the weather. You should see him tooling around in his convertible, Mr. Hollywood agent. Yep, Rooster's great. Everything's great, it really was. Bruce said to say hello.

The wedding?

The wedding was going to be a small affair. They were hoping to do a European honeymoon. As long as Bruce got his license. Did he know Bruce was studying to be an insurance broker?

"Would it be okay," he said as he brought the scotch to his lips, "if I walked you down the aisle?"

Laney knew, as it was unfolding, this scene was their last. So she waited. She took a peanut from the bowl, chewed it. "You've been gone so long, Dad." He nodded his head. Once.

Fuck it, I'm allowed to have a few tears in my eyes?

He saw and responded. Reaching across the table he took her hand. Bruce's pledge, a simple solitaire illuminated the space between them.

"Why, Daddy?"

"It was more than I could handle."

"What does that mean?"

He took a moment to gather his thoughts. "It was just too much for me."

And with that he let go.

"I think my dad dried and powdered."

Bruce rolls over, puts his arm around Laney, and pulls her into him. "What the fuck is wrong with you?"

"Nothing," she answers, snuggling in closer, "nothing at all."

"Come on." Bruce places his hand on Laney's shoulder. "Tell me."

Laney begins to play with the ends of her hair. "You're going to laugh at me."

Bruce turns her face, forcing eye contact, "No I'm not."

"I just can't stop thinking about the fact that none of this matters. Like tonight I was baking a cake with Janey and she was upset that it wasn't perfect and I wanted to tell her not to worry about it—that it didn't matter because nothing matters. We're all going to die. And when we're dead no one will ever know we ever made this cake. But then I remembered what it was like to bake a cake when I was her age so I stopped myself."

"I know you're resistant but you need to get help, honey. You're drinking too much. Not sleeping at night."

"I've never been a good sleeper."

"You can give me any excuse you want. I know one thing. It's not normal to be having these thoughts.

"Look around." Bruce spreads his arms. "Look at how lucky we are."

"That's the problem. When I look around I can't help but think about how it's all going to fall apart."

"MA!" ELI SHRIEKS.

Then again. Louder. Frantic. "Maaaa—"

Laney leaps from her bed, barrels down the darkened hall. She pushes through his bedroom door, takes him into her arms and holds him.

They were, he says between sniffles, walking down a city street.

"We were walking down a city street."

She was wearing headphones.

"You were wearing headphones."

They were walking down a city street together. They were on their way to meet Daddy. She was wearing headphones and he was trying to tell her something. To warn her.

But she didn't hear him, couldn't. Because she was listening to something else, "Something more important I guess."

Laney brings a tissue to his nose. "Blow, honey."

"I tried, Ma."

He blows.

"I shouted, 'Ma.'"

And again. More slowly the second time, "Ma…"

Nothing. No response.

An inexplicable, inarticulate stillness had fallen between mother and son. There were cars, moving cars. Walking, talking people. But there was no noise. He tried to reach for her, but couldn't. "It was like I was trapped."

And it was cold, colder than it was in real life. It was winter. It was winter, they were walking down a city street and she was wearing headphones. Laney didn't hear her son, didn't see the man approach, didn't feel the impact. She was, simply, dead.

Eli runs through all of it, his voice shaky, his body wet with sweat. "You didn't hear me, Mom." It is night, the middle of the night.

"That can never happen, honey." Laney pulls him closer.

He asks her how. "How do you know that can never happen?"

She decides she should bring humor into it. Isn't this what Bruce would do? "Because I don't have an iPod." She kisses the top of his head.

But this isn't what he wants, "That's not funny," he says drawing back.

"It can't happen because I won't let it happen." Laney is surprised by her emphatic tone.

"You can't control what happens."

"Yes, I can." She strokes his forehead. There are two basketball trophies on the shelf by his bed, a ping-pong certificate pasted to his dresser, a pile of wrestling action figures on the floor.

"I couldn't save you," he says again, one last time before drifting.

He always knew, her boy. The day he was born he knew.

He got the joke.

She placed his mouth to her nipple. He latched on, only to fall off. She readjusted her body to make it more comfortable for him.

"What's wrong, baby?"

But it wasn't a question of positioning. He looked at her, his eyes filled with compassion. It was as if he'd done this a million times before. As if he knew she needed permission to continue.

"You did save me, buddy." Laney pulls the blanket up past his shoulders.

"Who's gonna save you?"

THE FISH TANK BUBBLES BUT OTHER

than that there's no noise. Laney pours herself a glass of vodka, drinks it down, pours another. Outside her kitchen window the world is unchanged.

It is dark out, but Laney can picture every object in her back yard. Straight ahead two rubber balls are floating in the pool. One blue, the other red. A rake is leaning against the fence. Next to it the helmet for Eli's scooter and an empty pot filled with dirt. Behind the shed is a pile of lumber which will be used for the tree house Laney's having built. There is a swing set, a trampoline, and a plastic playhouse to the left. A small vegetable garden to the right.

Laney takes a sip, searches her bag. She locates the coke, dips her pinky in, changes her mind. She doesn't want to get wired— all hyped-up and itchy. In fact, she wants just the opposite—to take the edge off. She needs to calm down, to sleep; it's three in the fucking morning. She takes two Xanax from the pill case in her bag, pours herself another glass of vodka. No, she doesn't want to go to sleep.

Laney taps the remainder of the cocaine onto the kitchen table. She reaches for the pile of mail. Bills, catalogs, magazines. She sorts, tosses, glances out the window. It is dark, but not as dark. She cuts the cocaine with an envelope, lowers her head, inhales.

Night retreats, makes way for dawn. Dawn, first light, bright light. God. There is that—always. The looming question.

Laney opens her new *Vogue*—the extra thick fall-fashion issue. She turns the pages, wondering how it happened. That she became this old. She thinks maybe it's better to die young than wrinkle. She hates herself for having these thoughts, so mundane, so cliché, so on every page of this magazine in her hands.

"Like Wayne," he said, helping her up into the saddle.

Laney laughs at the memory, a quiet, timid little laugh. To think she fell for a line like that. She pictures her Cowboy's apartment above the stall, hard wooden floors, no blanket. Amazing that it didn't smell like shit up there, above all those horses.

Her house smells like shit. Every fall. Laney doesn't know why it backs up, but they fix it somehow, mother fucking shit-cleaner-uppers pull into her driveway, pinpoint a sod-covered access; roll out their giant hose. Shit's gone, an hour, maybe less.

She could call John Wayne. Right now. Talk rendezvous and love. He'd assure her that things aren't always as absolute as they seem. She'd say it was nice to hear his voice. And it would be nice—to hear his voice.

Until it wasn't.

It's easy, Laney knows, to get angry at what can't change. It's even easier when you don't really want it to. Really, what would Cowboy do with her full-time—linger outside the bathroom door as she freed herself from debris? It won't be all that she holds. It's never all.

Laney closes the magazine, throws her feet up on the table, leans back into the chair. She examines the panorama of her life: the chintz cushions, striped wallpaper, her collection of lunchboxes. She focuses, for a moment, on the one with Andy Gibb. *Fucking Andy Gibb.* The familiar rush comes on, tingling and numb. *Guy wasn't even a Bee Gee.*

LANEY HOPES THINGS WILL BE DIFFERENT

for her daughter. Janey can be an astronaut. She can be an astronaut, a scientist, a Peace Corps volunteer. A doctor, lawyer, nun. She can procreate on foreign soil: London, Calcutta. Or Janey can decide not to reproduce. Laney's daughter can be more, more than what she comes from, certainly more than her mother is.

Laney opens the door to her daughter's bedroom. Hope is not something she considers for herself. Hope is too abstract and she doesn't trade in abstractions anymore. Laney is into actualizing. Concrete fucking in-my-hands-right-here-where-I-can-palm-it. She fixes her eyes on her old Winnie the Pooh Bear, walks across Janey's room and grabs him. Brushing a piece of lint off Winnie's forehead, she brings him to the ground.

They face each other, a woman and her childhood bear. Eye to eye, lip to lip. She doesn't speak, merely kisses—one kiss, the scarred remains, a patch of black felt that once was his upper lip. She looks at him a last time before starting. If he said no she wouldn't do it, but he says nothing.

Upside down his stitched-together paws touch her just below her belly button. His head presses slightly against her pelvic bone. Laney lifts herself up over him and wiggles herself out of her panties. As she does this she focuses on a photograph on Janey's desk. She can make out everyone in the picture.

She eases herself onto the bear, presses the cool part of her crotch against Winnie's nose and begins rocking against him. She doesn't feel anything so she digs deeper, grinding her clit into Pooh's face.

Which shoes will she wear to drop Eli off at school today? Birkenstocks or clogs? Pumas? If she dresses down—Laney slides her cheek along the edge of a pillow, mouth open—it will make her less threatening. Pearls of sweat begin to form on the back of her neck. She keeps going, moisture builds between her legs, tingles start. *That's right. That's good.*

Laney checks to make sure Janey's sleeping. Poor thing, on her back, arms splayed, vulnerable. She glances at the bedroom door, it's open but just a crack. She squeezes her legs together, then squeezes tighter. She pictures her father, points her toes until both legs harden. She hears his voice, "Lane—Laney, honey."

She pushes harder into Winnie; now her dad's standing at some finish line, waiting for her. She's moving closer. *Yes, that's it.*

Laney continues toward him, kicking higher. *Do you? Do you? DO YOU LOVE ME?*

The quivering stops. Laney pulls Pooh out from under her. She rolls over onto her back, stares at the twinkling plastic stars that glow from her daughter's ceiling then closes her eyes. She's known this for a while, her whole life perhaps. How nothing bad needs to happen for her to feel sad.

Laney crawls, elbows and knees, down the dimly lit hall and into her bedroom. As she makes her way little beasts enter from behind, wiggling at her tail.

They say, "Honey, you're tired."

"Really?"

"Yes, you're tired."

Somehow this makes her feel old. "Are you saying I'm old?"

There is silence then. There is always silence then.

"I'm asking you," she says specifically, later over coffee, "are you saying I'm old?"

And this one laughs. Knowing he's going to leave. He laughs and says, "Of course not, honey."

He looks at her, right in the eye and promises her that she's still beautiful.

"Bruce?" Laney tugs at his blanket. "Bruce?"

He opens his eyes, "What are you doing down there?"

Laney's heart is pounding, racing. She looks at him, then turns away.

INTERMISSION

1

ON SUNDAYS, AT BLUE HILL HOSPITAL,
Managing Mental Health Since 1954
(detox, rehab, twenty-four-hours-a-day shrinkage)
Families visit.

Trying.
To deal with the swelling inside my head. I laugh at it. At who
I've become.
Cotton picker?
No.
Sharecropper?
Please.
Barney's shopper?
Ah-ha. Barney's shopper.
Am I grateful—
The nerve of me. Total disregard.

He sees it too. The man behind the counter.
He takes an exaggerated breath. Ladles gravy onto my
untouched turkey dinner.
He who doesn't know presumes.
Fair enough.

"You can have anything you want," Bruce assures me.
(A capitalist tendency)

But what I want.
(I don't say this, kids on either side).
He takes a bite, gestures his fork in the direction of my plate,
"Pretty good food they got here."
I use my fork to make swirly designs on the mashed potatoes.
"So what do you want? Name it."
"I don't know what I want."
But I do. To be left the fuck alone.
I want to be left the fuck alone, asshole. (Again I stop myself,
but this time it's not as easy.)

Shadows.
"I hate my shadow, Mom."
We are walking the grounds.
An afternoon stroll along hospital path.
Orange leaves. Pale blue sky.
"Why do you hate your shadow, hon?" My hand in his.
Arms swinging.
"Look—" He breaks free. Punches his foot into the other foot
on the pavement, "See how it won't stop sticking to me."

I'm left with a basket of fruit.
A transparent curtain, the fuzz on this peach.
My teeth sink into its flesh. Loosening skin from bone.
Me from you.
To believe again.
I pull back, smile.
You failed me, I think, then spit at it.

Deep breath.
I close my eyes and locate her.
Happy little dancer in her tutu.
Other's had visitors.

At lunch, the alcoholic at the table next to us (guy from Manhattan) shared a bowl of pudding with a three-footer in chin guards.

Across the room a young man with acne dined with his manic-depressive mom.

Imagine.

Eli, fourteen. Janey, twelve.

"Fuck," I say. Fuck, fuck, fuck.

And then I do what I do. I laugh again.

But it isn't a laugh I hear.

This is different.

This a howl.

And yet, if I were to cross against traffic I'd run.

ROOSTER FORRESTER, AGE EIGHT,

waits with marked uneasiness for his bus to arrive. Up and down West End Avenue boys of varying shapes and sizes pass time tossing balls in the air, kicking rubber-soled toes at blameless hydrants and biting their nails.

Alongside every child stands a designated adult liable for any and all mortifying acts of kindness, large or small, real or imagined. Accordingly, all waving, kiss-blowing, and sneaker-tying is prohibited.

"You sure you have enough to eat?" Rooster shakes his head at his mother and looks south. With any luck the yellow bus chugging up the street is his.

"And you have on sun block?" Again he nods his head. It's amazing. She simply can't help herself. Did he not give her a huge hug this morning, wolf down the entire plate of cheesy eggs she put before him, brush his teeth without her having to ask?

Rooster doesn't want to hurt his mother's feelings, but if he's driven to it he will. Mike Kalinsky flipped his mom the bird the other day. Rooster couldn't quite believe it, but he recognized why it was necessary. Once Mrs. Kalinsky started hollering after the bus, "Don't forget to use your inhaler, Mikey," there wasn't much the guy could do but give his mom the finger. Tough getting picked for teams when the captain knows you got asthma.

How many times, Rooster wonders, will his mom need it spelled out before she finally gets it? At breakfast this morning his dad said, "If all Rooster wants is a banana, Eileen, give the kid a banana and forget about it. If he's hungry, he'll learn." And still she stuffed his lunch bag.

Rooster looks at his mom clutching today's rejections: a turkey sandwich, Fritos, a frozen Charlston Chew. He wants to smile at her. She's cute, standing there in a Yankee t-shirt. But if he smiles, she may take it wrong, mistake his smile for solicitation and embrace him.

If that happened, Rooster would be forced to push her off him before the guys on the bus saw. And he doesn't want to do that, hurt her feelings. Because even with the newfangled conventions of boyhood—the indifferent shrug of the shoulder, the glib "whatever," the dismissive eye roll—even with all that, this brown-eyed, stiff-jawed third baseman loves his mother.

The distant yellow bus gradually approaches, then stops. The doors swing open and Rooster, armed with a single banana, his lefty mitt, and an unopened tube of sun block, climbs on. His mom delivers a reserved "hello" to Andy the bus driver and Coach Blauner. She then, as per her husband's instructions, sinks her fingers in her pockets, takes a step back from the curb and waits, without saying another word, for the doors to close and the bus to drive away.

Eileen remains this way for quite some time. A minute, maybe longer. She might, if she could, keep on there the whole day. Hang around until her boy is delivered home. If that's all she had to do to secure his safety, my goodness she'd spend the rest of her life on the corner of West 76th. Rain. Shine. Sleet. Snow.

Suppose there was a way to negotiate your ending: Ten additional good years, one breast to cancer but neither kid breaks a bone, she'd sign on.

Maybe she'd be daring, ask for more, can't be much of a

penalty for putting your cards on the table. If God is God, he already knows everything you're holding.

The more Eileen thinks about it the more she's certain. If there were a means to haggle, she'd haggle. And, for once in her life, courageously. No low-balling.

Twenty years and feel free to do whatever you want with me. She wouldn't hesitate to make that arrangement. Both kids in college. Roger's liver miraculously intact.

But God doesn't work like that. Eileen knows this. God doesn't do negotiations. She sticks her key in the front door of her apartment building, turns the lock, and enters. Andy said he'd be dropping Rooster back around four-thirty. Eileen checks her watch: eight-seventeen. What's that give her? Eight, nine hours to kill?

She presses for the elevator and waits. The arrow above the elevator door monitors its slow decent. The doors open. Eileen smiles politely to her neighbors as they exit. She takes a mouthful of air, holds it—Everything is okay. It's not like Rooster is on his way to overnight camp. Rooster is on his way to day camp in Jersey. No big deal—Releases. Eileen pushes for her floor. Even so, imagine how much easier it would be, how much less she'd worry—Forget just her, picture how peaceful the entire world would be if a person were aware of their beginning and ending all at once.

Laney, her ten-year-old daughter, loves to hear about the day she was born. How her daddy held her on the way home from the hospital, her rosy cheeks, her honey-colored hair. She doesn't ask about distress in the birth canal, Eileen's c-section, and subsequent depression.

If death were woven into the fabric of one's story early on, it would cease being abstract. Death, like birth, would be relegated to detail. A date on the calendar, a snapshot complete with color.

Death is a manifestation, the complete and total embodiment

of fear. A world without fear would be peaceful. There'd be no need for deterrence. No need for chin guards and elbow pads. No need for sublimation of any sort. Forget psychiatrists and nutritional supplements.

Say Eileen knew she was going to die on December 28, 2024, after a long and protracted bout with leukemia, but her boy was going to arrive home safely today at half past four with a smile on his face, Laney will stay pretty, marry a nice boy, a provider, and Roger won't drink himself into a coma—Eileen might actually be able to sit back and enjoy her day.

There are options: two. Be present or numb out. Eileen chooses to numb out. She slinks into the bedroom, pops a Valium, and heads to the kitchen. She kisses Laney on top her head, pours herself a cup of coffee, and sits down with the paper.

Maud, their cleaning lady, is busy with the laundry. Laney's painting. Eileen lifts the mug of coffee to her lips and watches as her daughter spreads lines of color on a sheet of white paper. Red into yellow, green into blue, continuous.

Eileen skims the headlines. *Children Of The A-Bomb. Stunted Bodies and Lives.* No one tells you the truth. She turns the page. *Explosions Flood Watertown. Force Some People Out Of Homes.* No one warns you how scary it all is.

"You think?" Rooster peels back the skin of his banana and takes a bite. "You really think they'd just let Reggie go?"

It is lunchtime at Camp Contender. Countless boys, aged six to twelve, are sitting on top a small hill just to the side of the ball fields. Most of the fields are covered—or if not covered, it's certainly fair to say well coated—with mud. The fields, not yet dry after the recent rains, are wet and slippery.

The hindrance, while noted, did little to discourage yet another morning of fierce competition between Mike Kalinsky's

Blue Jays and Rooster Forrester's Sun Cats. At noon, the score remains three runs to two. Sun Cats.

"Definitely." Mike bites into his turkey sandwich. "You think Steinbrenner. Forgot what he said about him."

"But he won them a series." Rooster holds firm. "Can't happen."

"You really think Steinbrenner cares about baseball? It's all about the money. It's a business, Roost." Willy Richter, arguably the best eight-year-old hitter to ever play at Camp Contender, is face deep in a bag of Doritos. Even so, his conviction resonates.

Rooster shakes his head, steadfast, "I just don't think they'd do that to the fans."

Mike reaches into Willy's bag and helps himself to a chip. "Rooster, you're the only person left in America who thinks wrestling is real."

Rooster, accustomed to this kind of coaxing from his friends, takes it in stride, "Bruno Sammartino would never throw a fight," he says, peeling down to his final bit of banana. Just then and for absolutely no apparent reason, Mike lunges at Rooster. Rooster reaches for his head but he's too late, his cap sailing through the air.

"Got it." Scottie Hathaway, another buddy of theirs, catches the cap and sprints down hill toward outfield. Rooster drops his banana peel on the grass and chases after Scottie. Scottie wouldn't do that, would he? Stick his cap in the mud?

By the time Rooster reaches third his cap is airborne again. Mike receives it at home, passes it off to Grady Miller. Now Grady, Rooster thinks, might very well sink his cap. After all, Grady's pissed. Rooster threw him out at first this morning, cost him a hit.

"There is," Rooster says to himself, "nothing special about that cap." He has several Yankee caps just like that one. Rooster knows he should be handling this differently. Not loping around after it, arms flailing in the air.

But Rooster wants his cap back. He wants his cap back and he wants to cry and not necessarily in that specific order. He is confused. Why would Mike steal his cap? And why would Scottie and Grady follow him?

"Because they're jealous of you," Eileen says, carrying a casserole to the table.

"That's what you say about everything, Mom."

"I say it because it's true. Ask your father. Isn't that why, Roger?"

Roger doesn't respond. Instead he watches his wife move effortlessly between the kitchen and dining room. Faithful she is, that a roast chicken will keep her family safe.

"Kids are no different than the adults they grow into." Eileen hollers from the kitchen. "People get threatened and Mike—" She is back in the dining room with the broccoli "—has been the most popular boy since kindergarten. He doesn't want you, Roost, or anyone else for that matter, to usurp his position.

Eileen is out the door again but quickly returns with a plate of watermelon wedges. She settles at the table, places her napkin on her lap, "What do you think, Lane?" Laney shrugs her shoulders, her eyes moving in the direction of her brother.

"That's not it, Ma. It's because I'm weak."

"Weak?" Eileen repeats. From the mystified tone in her voice one would think this is the first time Eileen ever heard the word.

"Who gave you that idea?" Roger reaches for the watermelon.

"Willy said it. Coach Blauner blew the whistle and as we were walking back to the dugout Mike tossed me my hat. Willy was with him and they were both kind of laughing and Willy said,

'You know why it's fun to tease you, Rooster, because you're weak.'"

"I want to rip the skin off those two little—"

Roger looks to his wife, then to his daughter, and finally to his son. He finishes chewing, spits a watermelon seed onto his plate, and folds his hands.

"Laney, honey, go into your brother's room, get one of his baseball caps and meet us in the living room. And Eileen, I need you to come join me on the couch."

Roger motions Eileen to get going then puts his arm around his son's shoulder and escorts him to the living room. His daughter, God bless, returns with not any cap but a Yankee cap.

"Thank you, honey." Laney, proud that her job had been well executed, plops herself on the window seat in the far corner of the room and begins picking at her toenails.

"Now, Eileen," Roger says as he puts the cap on her head, "I'm going to swipe this off your head and when I do I want you to chase after me." Roger waits to make sure he has secured both his wife's and son's attention. He then, as forewarned, swipes the baseball cap from his wife's head and begins running around the room with it. He dodges Eileen at every turn, over the piano bench, through the pocket doors, down the hall and back into the living room. This continues until the point is noted: Eileen will never catch him.

"Okay," Roger says, tossing Eileen the cap. "Now this time when I take the cap don't react, just stay in your seat as if nothing's happened."

Eileen resumes her position on the couch. She has always done this well, his wife, always been more than willing to follow his lead. Like the time Rooster soared over the handlebars of his bike and smacked face-first onto the concrete pavement. "You need to stay calm," Roger instructed Eileen as they ran to Rooster.

And she did it. No hysteria. Eileen cradled Rooster's head in her arms, stroked his hair as they waited for the ambulance to come.

Again, with sleight of hand, Roger swipes the Yankee cap from his wife's head. He circles the living room, begins thumping into walls for dramatic effect. Laney giggles, and per instruction, Eileen doesn't move.

"See, Roost," Roger says. "When Mom doesn't chase me all I am is a goofy guy staggering around his living room with a Yankee cap." Rooster's lips begin to curl. Roger squats before his son. "Something only has the value that you give it."

He hands Rooster his cap and turns. "And as for you, young lady"—Laney looks up but it's her mother her father is addressing—"there will be no ripping skin off any eight-year-old boys. Boys have been stealing each other's hats long before the Dodgers ever thought about leaving Brooklyn."

Later, and only after all dishes have been cleared from the table and put away, does Roger allow himself to acknowledge his feelings. He pours himself a tall glass of scotch, notes the pile of papers on his desk, the few scattered bills. They can wait, he tells himself, making his way across the room. He glances at Laney's painting. How funny, he thinks, noting the color. His daughter's interpretation of pretty the same as her mother's.

Roger sinks into his leather chair. This is his favorite time of day, both children tucked safely in bed, Eileen taking her bath. He eases farther, closes his eyes. This, his process, persevere, and then collapse. Act then reflect. Make your kid laugh, then fall apart.

o

Dr. Page, Laney's psychiatrist at Blue Hill, waits a beat, allowing the air in the room to settle. He couldn't be more than a year or two older than her. Fresh, eager, ready to repair.

"So why this story?" he asks.

Laney looks at the gold ring around his finger. Three days, three days in the outside world she'd have his heart.

"It's silly," she says, pushing her hair back behind her ear, "I don't know. Let's forget about it."

"That's a cop out."

"It's not even about me really."

"So why tell it?"

Laney sits straighter. "Why?"

"Yeah, if it's not even about you why did you bother to tell it?"

Laney glances out the window at the yellowing autumn leaves. It's three-thirty in the afternoon, the kids home from school by now. So many things she hadn't bothered chasing after. She pulls at a cuticle on her thumb.

"Cause I believed him." Her voice breaks just slightly.

"What does that make you?"

"What do you mean?"

"You said you and your brother are the embodiment of that hat to your dad. Something not worth fighting for."

Laney nods.

"So I'm just wondering. If you are a hat, what kind of hat are you?"

Through a thin veil of tears Laney smiles, "Red Sox, I guess."

2

LANEY'S BEEN GRANTED PERMISSION.

A field trip.

Bruce drives through the hospital gates. The rain tapping ever so gently against the windshield. Wipers on. Slow.

In the back seat their little girl sleeps, head cocked, mouth open. The girl's breath lends fullness to the air, to this space between them. The girl is alive. They are, all of them, alive.

As he drives it becomes undone. Little by little, with each passing exit it begins to peel away. Metaphors come to mind, like an orange, an onion. This, the shedding of skin, her skin. Here and now.

Laney, the vessel of self—the self she projects back onto him, her viewer. Look at me. You in the rearview mirror. Blue eyes. Open and alert. Coffee drinker.

They are, the two of them, bound. The outer him, the inner her. He is the more honest of the two? Maybe. But Laney's the braver one. Buckled in, back seat, safety locks.

Bruce insists that Blue Hill is for her own good. That Laney, chin up, should continue on course: twelve days of sobriety, people to talk to. This road a highway, he promises. Straight, long, flat.

The good girl, once more, Laney plays the part. Allowing him to manage the choices she makes. "You look like you're doing much better." This, in order to justify said directive.

He who never has to go to the party embodies her whole.

Faithful that her hair will cover his eyes just long enough to—
Naive motherfucker. She can turn on him. Any day. Fuck him up.
She can cut those eyes he uses, scoop them, loose. He is hidden
because she lets him hide. And only.

Awake now, the girl's pigtails wag back and forth. Husband
smiles, reaches for wife's hand. "This," he says, "is why we
continue." This handholding. But she knows it's a deception. In
the other ear he whispers, "Forever," then laughs.

There are questions. Was she always like this or did she
become? Fear. A heckler at the door. Around every corner.
Under the brush.

Each breath.

The struggle itself a conceit.

Still, if they are to be a family again, then together they
must acknowledge, Bruce must, the midget with the beard.
"Remember when Eli saw that little person in the market and
thought he was a boy cause of all those commercials and said,
'That boy must watch television because he's paying with a Visa
check card.'" Laney looks at Bruce. This time it's he who looks
away.

Of all people. Turn, reverse, park. Who said the sun was sure
to come out. That Janey would love this, all little girls love. Tell
her then, why does the darker possess the beauty? And also, why
didn't Eli come to visit?

This morning, after family meeting, two icy glasses of water
pressing together, Bruce said, "The problem with dying, Lane,
is that once you die you're dead."

Did she? No, Laney bent her lips. Passed the maple syrup.
Bruce makes distinctions.

Today's face at the carousel stands beneath a green and
white striped umbrella. He gums then rips their tickets. How to
continue? Black hole. Gold teeth. Bacteria crawls. As she, cut
open, rubbed out, remains. Head down, staring at her feet.

Laney lifts her daughter onto a horse. Threads strap, pulls

through, holds on from behind. The music starts. Around they go. But a formation, a contortion, a meal.

Laney asks, keeps, if she needs to return by a specific time and still no answer. Why the mystery?

"THAT'S NOT TRUE," MARISSA SAYS.

"Your dad loves you a lot." Three girls, two in training bras, are sitting Indian Chief style on Marissa Gordon's top bunk. Rebecca Gordon, Marissa's little sister, is allowed to participate in the upcoming séance, even without the extra support, for the following reasons:

–Three people are needed to conduct a proper séance.

–Laney likes having Rebecca around.

–It is, no disputing, Rebecca's room too.

Even with such concessions, Laney's downstairs neighbor Marissa Gordon reigns supreme. She is the older sister and thus, not only in possession of the top bunk and better scrapbooks —diligently documented first steps, first words, first haircuts compiled by her compulsive but kind mother, Lucy—Marissa Gordon, chestnut hair, green eyes, braces on both upper and lower teeth, is the self-anointed spiritual leader of the trio.

It must be stressed, here and now, that Marissa is and has always been prone to believing: the tooth fairy, red sequined shoes, the Sleeping Beauty. So the idea that at thirteen she'd be conducting a rather sophisticated beckoning of the spiritual world isn't a surprise as much as a natural progression.

Also important to note, the Gordon girls have recently returned—recently, as in the night before—from overseas. Their father, Mr. Gordon, charged with opening the London branch of an esteemed Rock and Roll-themed café, had transported his family to London for the school year.

While there, Marissa entered into a relationship with a boy from California, a sophomore named Kyle Thurm. Kyle, the son of some famous Transcendentalist at Oxford was kind enough to introduce Marissa to the spiritual edification of the Ouijui which Marissa claims allowed her to converse with John Lennon and actually have tea, Chamomile mind you, with Princess Grace.

("But my dad isn't dead," Laney said when Marissa introduced the idea.)

("The spiritual world isn't exclusive to the dead," Marissa's answer.)

Kyle was also kind enough to guide Marissa through the merits of a pinner versus a fatty. And lastly, but certainly of no lesser importance, there were Kyle's lessons, which Laney was sure to "benefit from" (Marissa insisted) on the art of a good hand job.

So it is with absolute authority that Marissa Gordon proceeds to take inventory: "Incense?" The Gordons have been Laney's downstairs neighbor for as long as she can remember. Their close proximity has much to do with the core understanding of their friendship. Morning after morning, years, in fact, spent see-sawing at the park, sharing cold grilled cheese sandwiches, tossing their crusts to birds, have lent their friendship a particular tone, a fluidity that's been able to transcend divergent opinions about music, movies, and now the afterlife.

"What scent?" Marissa asks.

"Frankincense," Laney answers with noticeable hesitation. "Frankincense was all the store had."

"Frankincense is fine," Marissa reassures and then, like a surgeon crying out for scalpel just before making an incision, Marissa summons, "Candles."

Rebecca brings forth three candles, two white and a purple

one for added spirituality. "Great," the older sister says, placing them on the tray table between them. Then, with a wave of her hand she motions said deputy who in turn flings herself over the top bunk and flicks off the last remaining light.

From up here, the room below seems far away, almost pretend. Laney feels, incense burning, candles glowing, as if she is floating on a magic carpet, in Wonka's glass elevator, with Peter Pan. In fact, she is sure she is floating. Close enough to touch the ceiling's sponge-painted sky. Only a tap on the talking board—a talking board carried, by hand, all the way from London, England, could convince her otherwise.

"Let's begin." Marissa extends her arms, the three girls lock hands. "Dear God, thank you for bringing us here and for giving us the power of the Ouijui." Laney breathes in through her nose, out through her mouth as instructed. She does this several times, all the while concentrating, per Marissa's instructions, on the candles. "Focus on the peaceful smoke rising from the candle's white flame." Rebecca props her head on her fingertips, her conviction fierce enough to compensate for Laney's lack of visual acuity.

"There are several steps to ingratiating those that have left us." (Marissa waits for Laney to acknowledge the clever use of word choice, which Laney does by shrugging her shoulders, and continues.) "Close your eyes and picture something peaceful, something about your dad that made you happy."

Three days before Laney's dad left, he took her for a carousel ride in Central Park. Looking back, she might have pegged it strange, Dad taking her there and all. It wasn't like it was a birthday or anything. He must have known then, that he was leaving.

Laney follows Marissa's coaching, closing her eyes, bowing her head. That was it; the last time she remembers being happy. Only happy.

"Do you remember your first time?" he said as they entered.

"It was your brother's eighth birthday. He had his new bike with him. You were on my shoulders and when you saw this carousel you nearly fell off. Mom was hysterical but you didn't seem to notice. 'Horsey' you kept shouting, 'Horsey, Daddy.'"

This, and the story of when her mom and dad met were Laney's favorites. So familiar were her responses to the ebb and flow of Dad's dialogue they appeared scripted.

Laney took his hand. "So we asked your brother to pull over, which he did, despite being worried that someone might steal his bike."

Dad passed the gatekeeper two yellow tickets, "Do you remember any of this, Lane?"

"Of course, Daddy."

They circled the carousel in search of two vacant horses.

"We almost missed our turn, Lane. We had to walk around like three times until you found exactly the right horse. Finally you stopped and pointed to a horse and said, 'this one.'"

At the far side of the carousel stood two vacant horses. "'There, Daddy,' you said, walking in the direction of the horse with a turquoise saddle."

Her father climbed on to his horse and looked at Laney, "And when I asked you why, what did you say?"

Laney remembers looking at her father then. His cheeks hard in comparison to the soft curves of her own. "Because it had happy eyes. Three years old and you were already talking about…"

"Laney!"

Rebecca is pulling at Laney's shirt.

Laney opens her eyes. "Did you hear him, Laney?" Laney wants to say yes, to pacify them, but if she opens her mouth she might start to cry—she doesn't want to cry.

Marissa raises her hands up over her head. "You still with us, Mr. Forrester?"

There is a knock on the board.

"What do you want to ask him, Laney?"

Laney motions with her hands as if to say please, Marissa, you talk.

"Sometimes," Marissa says with compassion, "the presence of the spirit silences us."

"Mr. Forrester!" Marissa begins rocking back and forth, "Roger Forrester, what do you have to say to your daughter?" Laney glances over at Rebecca, who up until that moment appeared pretty cool about the whole thing. All color has drained from her cheeks and it appears, at least to Laney, like Rebecca might faint.

The younger girl's uneasiness burns a hole through Laney's chest. Laney wants to take Rebecca into her arms, reassure her that there's nothing to be scared of, that there are no such things as ghosts. And furthermore her father isn't dead. He's alive and well, somewhere in Boca, walking distance from the ocean. If he had any interest in speaking to Laney, all he'd have to do is call.

"But Marissa—" Laney looks at her friend gyrating back and forth, the velocity of her body rivaled only by her intention. Laney looks at her and realizes, perhaps for the first time, how much this whole thing, her father leaving like he did, scares Marissa too. Marissa senses Laney looking at her and opens her eyes.

"He loves you, Laney. He told me to tell you that, that he loves you."

Now, Laney knows her dad and if he were to make a cameo appearance in the room it wouldn't have been to say he loved her. He'd poke fun at them. Tease Marissa about her alleged hand-job prowess. Tell Rebecca to make some cool friends. Maybe he'd say something to Laney like, "Good going—nothing like burning candles on the top bunk."

Laney tries her best to smile. In this short period of time she has become good at this, at smiling in order to discharge. People need it, permission to return to their happy little lives. Even a girl brave enough to summon her upstairs neighbor's missing father needs to turn the lights on, brush her teeth, and get ready for bed.

o

"Why didn't you ever call him? You could have, right? Called him."

"Yeah," Laney answers, "I could have called him."

"So why didn't you?"

"I couldn't do that to my mother."

"Do what?"

"Betray her like that."

"Would it have been a betrayal to call him?"

"Wouldn't it have been?"

"But your mom was re-married, happily, according to you."

"People do all sorts of things in order to survive."

"Come on, Laney."

"It sounds so silly now."

Quiet.

Laney looks across the room at him. Patient, Dr. Page. Look at him: sitting in his chair, hands folded, determined.

"What if he didn't answer the phone?"

3

"WHAT WERE YOU THINKING THAT

afternoon?" Bruce came alone today. A white oxford shirt with a narrow navy stripe.

"Which afternoon?"

"When you ran the red."

"Nothing."

They are in the Blue Hill cafeteria having lunch. "You were thinking nothing?" Bruce bites into his sandwich.

"Nothing more than, well, I guess I thought if I closed my eyes, plowed through that red, and was hit by another car—you're going to laugh."

"No I'm not."

Laney's hands are folded. Her posture straight. "I thought I'd know what God wants for me. If I'm supposed to live or die."

"And now what?" Bruce looks at her with wide, innocent eyes.

"Now?"

"Yeah, now that you know the answer."

His question is matter-of-fact. As if the thoughts in her head can be flicked on and off at will. "There's a way you want me to answer this, right—and if I give you the answer you want then you'll take me home?"

"Do you want to come home?" Bruce doesn't mean for this to offend her and she knows this. Still, Laney can't help herself.

"You're just another fucking coward, Bruce."

He puts the sandwich down, wipes his mouth on the napkin, and reaches for both her hands. "Why are you so angry?"

"I'm not angry," Laney says, fighting back tears. She continues to look at him, her silence deliberate.

"Tuck those doughnuts in your pockets, guys, it's starting to rain."
"I love running in the rain with you," Eli shouts.
"Me too, Mommy." Laney stops, looks at them. These, her children.
"Jump!" she says and they leap over a small puddle.
Dashing through rain with abandon.
Laughing, without fear.

"What is it then?"

She slips her hands out from within his. "I'm scared."

"What are you scared of, specifically?"

Looking across the table at him sitting there in a collared shirt she's almost sorry but not entirely. "Of everything, Bruce, of every fucking little thing."

11 Watchung Road (four years prior)

"YOU ARE GOING TO BE SO HAPPY."

Bruce passes Laney a gold key tied with a red ribbon. She should respond but doesn't.

"What do you think?"

He doesn't get it yet, that she thinks nothing. Maybe *what the fuck.* If she thinks anything she thinks, *What the fuck—a big house to clean?*

Bruce walks round the car, opens the door, takes Laney by the arm. He is grinning, leading his wife down a cobblestone path to a red lacquered front door. "Isn't this what you always wanted?"

It is, in fact, what she had told him she wanted. A white house with black shutters, a red door. But those were the fantasies of a city girl. Laney looks at this house and wonders what she has left, if anything, to fill it with.

Inside, newly sheet-rocked walls stand erect. Unmarked by time or memory. Which is, Laney thinks, what makes these new constructions so appealing. Prewired: telephone, cable, computer. Nine-foot ceilings, recessed lighting, crown molding, and chair rails.

"Wait until you see this," Bruce says, prodding her into the kitchen. Laney focuses on the beige cabinets, the concrete countertop. She wonders how many hours it took, how many great minds to work this out. Double oven to the left, eight burners to the right.

A pair of French doors leads out back. On the patio is a

barbeque, a table, an umbrella. Laney gazes at the small lima-bean-shaped pool. Black-bottomed, it blends with the edge of the neighbor's wrought iron fence. "Can't do this in the city," Bruce is saying. "We'll have parties out back, barbeques. It's the perfect house, don't you think?"

Laney throws her arms around her husband's shoulders in an attempt to submit. "It sure is, babe."

Even so, her back propped against newly fitted planks, she is besieged. Fear cripples the outskirts of her heaven and she hates him for it. But let's say she were to let Bruce, his finger, tickle her clit longer. Same spot, farther distance. And if she responded, a fluttering, a release of breath, would that mean she loved him?

Bruce breathes on her, his smell habit. "You're so beautiful," he says. Eyes shadowed by heavy lids. Laney looks away, practiced but sincere. Rising to him, a timid gesture, "Really?"

She lifts deeper into it, engulfing his terrain. Her cunt, a partner in this exchange, asking-pleading him to tell her more.

The splinters, from the porch, itch her brain. Scattered teardrops evaporate in humid air. How she wishes to love him.

Simple, this peasant dance. Creatures in search of higher order. Bruce would tap. Laney's certain. In shiny shoes. Bereft, over a vacant soul. As plain as the light of day, the hollow ground beneath him. He would deny its existence, argue it.

"Look at me," he'd offer, his feet sliding along a transparent floorboard. But not her. Feet fastened. Utterly inevitable, opaque, her grief.

The lights dim, allowing darkness to illuminate a single heroic gesture. "Hello New York"—the crowd cheered and they rocked. Father. Daughter. Popcorn. Cotton candy.

Laney remembers thinking, even as a child, that there was something wrong with Anka's smile. She wasn't able to place it back then although now she can spot a toothy grin before a guy even has the chance to smile. *Having my baby, what a lovely way of saying how much I love you.* Anka left for his masseuse.

Angry that the hair on Bruce's chest is no longer only black,

Laney accounts what was. Remembrance, like pure love, a conceit. This learned at an early age. She shrugs, presses through air heavily laden with debris. How she longs to swim. Arms stroking water, thick as syrup.

Naked before her reflection she spars. A layering of wrinkles destined to rot. All of us. *Even you with the mighty tits.* She tells that voice to go away, to, "Shut the fuck up."

Laney pictures her dad. Silk shirt, yellow tie. Polished. Refined. She is, if anything, him. Just. Chisel-cheeked. Cruel.

And this is when she breaks. Diving into the pool. A cloudy film before her eyes. Regret impotent within a chlorinated body. There she goes. One arm in front of the other, bound to destroy.

Ubiquitous, the stranger. His arms a cave. Laney burrows in, seeking safety. Dress up easy, she glides. Chin up toward heaven, pussy saturated with hope.

With Bruce she is clumsy. It is, all of this, too real. She can't let him do this, own her. Not again, never again will a man own her. She kicks out.

"So you like your house?" he asks from the far side of the pool.

"Yes," she answers. Her voice anywhere but here.

She paddles toward him, places wet head on shoulder. "I really do."

o

"My mom says she only has one real regret in her life."

"What's that?"

"If she had to do it all over again she would have followed through with this summer job she had set up for herself at Disneyland. She worked her way up and was finally going to get to be a character. Do you know who Snow White is?"

Dr. Page smiles. "The fairest of them all."

Laney can't believe it, "How do you know that? I'm sorry— I'm probably not supposed to—"

"I'm happy to tell you. I have a daughter."

Laney takes a moment to process this. A daughter. Dr. Page is a father.

"Can I ask you what her name is?"

"Her name's Samantha but my wife and I, we call her Sam."

What would it be like to have someone like Dr. Page as a father, to have someone you could rely on?

"Sam's a nice name."

"Thanks." Dr. Page gestures for Laney to continue.

"So my mom was going to get to dress up every day and greet visitors at the gates to the Magic Kingdom."

"What stopped her?"

"She started dating my father and he had other plans." Laney pauses for dramatic purpose, raises her eyebrows. "There was a house in his picture." She shrugs her shoulders.

"Have you noticed it, how there's always a house?" Laney has tears in her eyes.

"You're going to be okay," Dr. Page says.

"You think?" It is time to go home. Bruce is waiting, engine on.

Dr. Page stands, walks over to the door, opens it. "If you let yourself."

Laney exits. One foot in front the other.

Jean jacket.

Cowboy boots.

Chin up.

Sunny day.

A Springsteen melody drifts through the open passenger window. Laney looks at her husband tapping his fingers on the steering wheel. He smiles at her. And to her surprise, without trying to, she smiles back.

ACT TWO
North Jersey
Five weeks later

LANEY IS ONE OF THEM AGAIN. A

mother with four hours to kill until pick-up. A housewife pushing a pig-tailed child, seated in the basket of a large red grocery cart, through the aisles of Joe's Party Palace. Busy hunting: for a glimmer in the eye, the curling of an upper lip, a bag of Snow White party hats. Laney needs a burst of joy, a gleeful tone. Needs to be brought back to, she doesn't know exactly, an early winter morning?

Must have been a Sunday cause her dad was there, motioning her to move away from the front door. He opened it, allowing the icy-cool air from outside to puncture the friendly temperature of their building.

He leaped, pajamas, no shoes, into a cool winter morning. Laney, worried that her dad's toes would freeze, he'd catch a cold, slip and break his arm, crept a step or two closer to the door: feety pajamas, Pooh bear. She stuck her head out. Amazingly, it took all but a second or two for him to reach the curb and grab the paper. "Get back in there, hon."

Laney, being a good little girl, jumped back inside, a big goofy smile on her face. That man out there, the handsome man making his way back to her, her dad, thirty-ish, with his dark hair, thin white pajamas, cold red toes was, is still perhaps, the love of her life. Or if not the love of her life, because she has other loves, her husband, her kids, then the embodiment of her love.

One flight up, in the limegreen kitchen of her earliest childhood her dad handed her the comics section of the paper and a mug of hot chocolate. Laney, just learning to read, asked for his help. He opened his arms, told her to scoot over: "Scoot over, pumpkin." She did this with ease. Eager, as always to be sheltered within his musty smell, his warmth.

Somewhere deep inside Laney marked this moment. She didn't know it then, how to articulate what she was feeling. It was magic, as inaudible and elusive as the meaning of life itself. Because it was, in many ways, the meaning of life itself.

Ironically, Laney has spent the majority of her adult life searching for the belief that came so easily as a child. Funny where she looked for it. She blew a few guys—not there. Shrooms, EX—*nada*. She got married, the veil, the gown—But it wasn't until yesterday's homecoming. Janey's outstretched arms were filled with a trust, a wanting so naive, so pure that it made Laney want to weep for days. *An innocent.*

She pressed her little girl against her chest. Miraculously, at that moment, Laney felt the very faith that eluded her.

Home from rehab in time to make both kids' Halloween costumes by hand, Laney will smile for the camera. Again she will feel it.

Meaning? A sense of value?

No, Dr. Page. It's not either of those things.

Look at Laney, marching up and down these aisles, her very own Joe's Party Palace credit card in her pocket. There's Janey's birthday to buy for, Halloween, the World Series.

Laney is motivated by hunger. Still an addict, she craves the high. A joyful birthday party. A winning pumpkin pie. These momentary escapes allow her to pretend. That it's all going to be okay. That she won't destroy.

Jonzing for another hit, Laney heads toward the back of the store. *Maybe Janey will light up from a piñata.* Laney points to a rainbow form with multi-colored streamers. "What do you think, cutie?"

"I love it, Mommy."

Laney grabs three bags of candy, a stick with gold tinsel, a small stuffed doggie with a foil crown on his head. She needs to feel it, whatever it is, or at least see it on Janey's face.

For sure it's in the red sequined party shoes Laney saw in the window of Smith's. She'll stop there, she reassures herself, on the way home, buy Janey a pair.

Click your heels and say—

Even better. She'll buy Janey a pair in every size they have.

There's no place like home.

Just in case Smith's loses their lease, gets bought out by a chain, closes up shop. Or the shoe manufacturer changes their mind and suddenly decides little girls are no longer in the market for red sequined party shoes.

Time, Dr. Page has taught her, needn't be limited to forward/backward progression. Time is strangely lateral, memory recorded in the fold of a page. Scenes can be added and subtracted arbitrarily. Like a slice of Jell-O mold, they take their own shape when removed from the whole.

Laney can make this part of her life anything she wants to make it. A couple weeks away is nothing in the scheme of things. At the very least she must honor her obligation. Gather enough strength to raise her kids with hope even though she herself exists in the fallout of that hope.

Because while it's true that forever is really a quantifiable term, that all daddies leave one way or another before their little boys and girls are ready for them to, that most newspapers have canceled their Sunday comics altogether, what's the alternative?

Run away to Boca?

Laney looks at Janey perched in the shopping cart, waving the tinsel wand. Beauty exists. Laney takes this in.

Deep breath.

Beauty exists. And therein lies the miracle, that it exists at all.

In the distance of Laney's mind, in memory, is the sound of laughter, her laughter. More a slurpy giggle than a deep chortle, it is the resonance of her own unmitigated joy. Every once in a while she lets herself hear. Sometimes it brings tears to Laney's eyes. Most of the time, though, she just nods back a thank you and keeps on going.

PEOPLE, HER HUSBAND, MOTHER,

girlfriends, shrink; insist she looks happy. Today at pick-up Diane tells Laney she looks "pretty" again.

"You look so pretty again," Diane says. Always with a qualifier. As if one has the right to tell another they look pretty "again" or pretty ever.

To the onlooker, the distance between Laney then and now is transitory: a bad haircut, a touch of acne, a boring matinee. This, as it should be. A match is always less significant for the spectator. Free to turn away, to grab a Coke, a hot dog with relish. To marry, remarry.

"At peace" is the other one.

"I agree," Wendy says. "You look at peace, Laney."

For the fuck of it, Laney is polite, utters, "Thank you," and smiles. They're so silly. As if peace can be procured: an option exercised, a transaction fulfilled.

They, the who that is "they," assume her looking "pretty" and "at peace" is because she's back home with her family.

And how lucky she is to have Bruce. I don't know if my husband would have put up with me checking into rehab for a month.

Or that she's taking medicine.

I heard the medicine she's on slows your metabolism so she's gaining some weight, thank God.

For them, a few manifestations of normalcy and she is whole, somehow.

People, Laney accepts, see what they want to see—believe

what they want to believe, regardless of what you show them to the contrary. But that's neither here nor there. What others think of her is not her problem. She has her ID hanging from her neck like the rest of them.

"Are you driving into the city tomorrow night, Di?"

"No, I was planning on taking the train. Andy's away. Why?"

"I'm meeting Bruce at the party so I thought I'd see if you could give me a ride."

"Take the train with me. We'll get to catch up."

Laney likes this idea, "Sounds perfect."

"Great. I'll pick you up around eight."

The classroom door opens. Laney spots her boy. Nets jersey, shaggy hair. There he is. She smiles at Eli and he begins to smile back—it's instinctive and unrefined, the love a child has for their parent—but stops himself.

She looks strange to him. She is too tall, too—

Eli readjusts his knapsack. He is buying time, although he doesn't know this, four-corner offense, that he is stalling. But he is. He's stalling because he doesn't know what to say to his mother. Not yesterday when she came home. Not today. "Hello"; "How are you?"; "Welcome home." Eli can't seem to utter the words. So he simply refuses without knowing it's a refusal.

Many years from now it will become a philosophical question. A tree falls in the forest and no one hears, did it fall? What is the sound of one hand clapping? If Eli never acknowledges his mother having left him for twenty-eight days, did she?

Right now all that matters is that she's here. His mother. Not Billie's or Jack's. Not his grandmother. His mother is here to pick him up. Flesh and bones. A beating heart.

Still, she looks strange to him. She is too tall, too—

He fights the thought. No she's not. She's beautiful. He looks around the classroom. She's the prettiest mom in the room. And she's here to bring him home.

Which is all that Eli wants. He wants his mom down the hall

from him at night, needs her to be. Without her there he feels lost. More than lost he feels unanchored. It's as if he's drifting and no one. Not Dad, not Skip the swim instructor, nothing but his mother's grip can pull him back to land.

"I'll hold it for you, honey." She's touching him now, hand on shoulder—but he doesn't want to be touched. Not by her. Not yet. Ever, perhaps.

Her smell, as familiar as his own, is processed: Secret deodorant, Lancôme skin cream, Fracas perfume. All of which can be purchased for $103.65. But to him, Laney's scent is singular. It is the smell of his mother. His. And yet he pulls away.

The knapsack drops off Eli's shoulder and she takes it from him. Together they walk alongside other mothers with other sons. Daughters. They are, him and his mom, what they appear to be, son and mother. And yet they are nothing that they appear to be.

This moment is one of many. It is a process, if not the process of childhood, it's certainly a determining factor of survival—the ease in which one is able to split their reality. There is the world as it exists, and then, just next to it, the world one creates in order to exist. The boundaries limited only by one's imagination.

Later it will become a psychological question. There are terms. Detachment? Dissociation? Trans-generational trauma reoccurrence? But for a long time, a lifetime perhaps, what Eli is about to do will become his mechanism of choice: suppress the anger, compensate with kindness, forget that he ever cried himself to sleep.

"I want to show you something, Ma." He reaches for his knapsack and Laney passes it back to him. Eli drops his bag on the sidewalk and begins digging.

"I made this for you." He passes her a hard object wrapped in blue tissue paper. Laney unwraps.

It is, other than her children's faces, perhaps the most beautiful thing she has ever seen.

"You made me a dream catcher?"

"Yep," he says zipping his bag. "No more bad dreams, Ma." Laney's not sure whose dreams he's referring to. His or her own.

"Yes," she says pulling her sunglasses down over her eyes. "That would be nice."

Laney drives.

From the back seat, Eli is busy explaining how ice cream is really a vegetable.

"If I can prove ice cream is really a vegetable can I get two scoops?"

"Sure."

"Well, Mrs. Stacker says milk comes from cows and cows eat grass—"

Laney nods.

"—And vanilla comes from a vanilla bean and sugar comes from cane plants and—"

Eager, Laney plays along. "I get it."

And she does. There's no denying everything is connected to everything else. She came from something ugly and broken… but so did Eli. Laney allows herself to entertain the possibility: Eli's essence—despite her being his mother—is beautiful somehow. Perhaps deep down hers is too.

Laney opens the car door and Eli hops out through the front. "I'm getting Rocky Road."

"Yum." Laney takes her boy's hand.

"What are you going to get, Ma?"

"I don't know."

"Get something different. Something that's not fat-free so I can share it."

"Share it! Aren't you getting two scoops?"

"Yep, but three would be even better."

All Laney wants is to feel normal. Never eating anything that isn't fat-free isn't normal. One scoop of regular ice cream. She can manage that. One kid-size scoop isn't the end of the world.

But Laney is scared she's getting fat. Her increased appetite is as real a side effect as the evening sweats, dry mouth, uneasy belly she gets from the medication Dr. Page's got her on.

One line. One joint. One drink. Anything?

She stops herself. And as far as she's aware, craving doesn't invalidate sobriety. There's a significant distinction. Because Laney's not, twenty-nine days sober, full of it or anything. She's endeavoring to the best of her ability. Look at her day: she took Janey to get birthday party stuff, remembered to pick up the dry-cleaning, and got to dismissal on time.

The door chimes as they enter. Ice cream. Even with the thirty-two flavors this is a simple proposition. Cone or cup? Topping? Rainbow sprinkles or chocolate? Eli runs ahead, presses his nose against the glass.

"Can I help you?"

Laney looks at the pimply-faced kid behind the counter. His reissued Guns N' Roses t-shirt is endearing.

"Sure. I'd like a very, very small scoop of chocolate, kid size."

"We don't do kid size for adults."

"I'll pay for a regular scoop just make it really small, okay?"

"Got it."

"And this guy here," Laney gestures toward Eli, "is going to have a scoop of Rocky Road and—" Laney waits for Eli to announce his choice but Eli doesn't. "E?" Laney asks, "What do you want, E? Rocky Road with what?" But still no answer.

"Excuse me a second."

Laney kneels, "What you doing, E?"

Eli is preoccupied. He has contorted his eyes in such a way

that it's hard to see their color. He continues to stare at something on the other side of the glass until he blinks. But it's not an ordinary blink. This is longer, harder, painful almost.

He does it again: contorts his eyes, stares blankly through the glass counter, squeezes his eyelids closed. Laney watches Eli do this two times more before saying anything. She asks again, more loudly this time, "E, what you doing?"

She's gotten his attention.

"Just straightening out the lines."

"What lines?"

He is bewildered by the question. "The lines! Look at the ice cream, Ma. See how the edges of the containers don't connect to each other? And look at the door; see how the door is crooked? If I do this with my eyes—he rolls them up into his head, holds them there, blinks hard—I can even everything out."

Laney takes a deep breath. He wasn't doing this before she went away, was he?

"You know, E, straightening out all the uneven lines in the world—that's a big job for a guy your age."

Eli shrugs his shoulders.

She did this to him. Laney's certain. She made him crazy.

The guy in the Guns N' Roses t-shirt passes Laney her chocolate cone. "So did he decide?"

Laney looks to her boy.

"I'd like a scoop of Rocky Road and a scoop of vanilla, please." And somehow in the blink of an eye, literally, Eli is a normal boy again.

It doesn't matter though. His voice, Laney thinks, will change sooner than later. And with this thought Laney takes a lick and swallows.

LANEY TIGHTENS THE LID ON THE JAR

of cream. "Right arm," she says, helping Janey into the nightie.

"Tell me a bed night story, Mommy." Janey snuggles beneath the covers.

"Okay. I'll tell you a story, Janey, but then you have to close your eyes and go straight to bed. It's late."

"Okay, Mommy."

Laney places her head on Janey's pillow and holds her from behind. "Well, once upon a time there was a very ugly princess named Blanche. She was so ugly that people could hardly look at her. One night she decided that what she would do is steal all the diamonds from the sky and put them on a necklace. With a necklace so bright, no one would notice her chapped lips, crackly skin, beady little eyes.

"So late that night, she climbed on top the roof of her SUV and plucked all the stars from the sky. She put them, one by one, into a velvet sack. Then, as if it were a perfectly ordinary evening, Blanche went about her bedtime ritual."

"What does that mean, Mommy?"

"*Ritual* means the things you do all the time. Like how you brush your teeth before bed. Anyway, that night Blanche took a long and quite luxurious bubble bath, toweled off and began, as she did every night, to apply a very expensive face cream from Bergdorf Goodman, the fanciest department store in New York City. Finished, she crawled into her princess bed, pulled her Egyptian cotton sheets up over her shoulders, and closed her eyes. Blanche always made sure to get at least eight hours of beauty rest.

"The next morning she woke up bright and early, wrapped her miserable face in a colorful silk scarf, covered her eyes with glamorous dark sunglasses and made her way over to Franz Finkelfarb, the jeweler.

"Franz couldn't believe his eyes. He had never seen diamonds as pretty as these. 'My goodness, Princess Blanche. These sparkle like stars.'"

"Because they were stars," Janey says excitedly.

Laney smiles, tucks Janey's hair behind her ear, continues.

"Meanwhile, in a small and not very glamorous apartment on West End Avenue lived the hero of our story. A little girl named"—the name takes Laney a second to conjure—"Pinky Tinkerbink."

"Pinky Tinkerbink," Janey repeats, enthralled.

"Yes, Pinky Tinkerbink. Pinky was sweet and smart and she had these great big blue eyes through which she saw the world in all its wonder."

"What does that mean?"

"She noticed everything that was pretty."

"Did she like flowers?"

"Yes. Pinky Tinkerbink loved flowers."

"Like me."

"Just like you—flowers and cotton candy—she even had a collection of tiny glass animals like you do. But on this day, Pinky was very sad. Late last night, when she looked out her bedroom window, all the stars were gone, the sky was black. This could only mean one thing. Without a star to wish on, her dream could never come true. She would never have two pretty hands like all the other girls in school.

"Just yesterday her good friend Katie Meyers made fun of her. 'You look like Captain Hook,' she said and laughed. And another friend, Abby Ross, actually got up from the lunch table a few weeks ago and told the teacher that she had to switch seats. The sight of Pinky's finger while she ate made her want to throw up."

"That's so mean."

"Of course it's mean. But not any meaner than Fannie teasing you about your glasses. Kids are sometimes mean."

"Why?"

"All different reasons. But I think part of it is that kids get scared when something's different. And Pinky's left pinky didn't look like anyone else's. It was metal and shaped like a thin, jagged rod."

"Why did she have that?"

"She was born that way. Of course Pinky's mommy and daddy kept telling her that one day she'd see, it's not the hand that matters, it's what you do with it. Still, it was getting harder and harder for Pinky to wait for that one day. And now there were no stars."

"Oh," Janey says, raising a small, delicate, and completely formed hand to her mouth in a meager attempt to hide a yawn.

"That's a perfect place to stop."

"No, Mommy. Finish the story."

"Okay, but then you have to promise me you'll close your eyes and go right to sleep."

"Promise!"

"Well, the next day Pinky was moping on the couch, staring at her ugly finger when she noticed something unusual."

"What?"

"There was writing on it."

"What did it say?"

"It said, Citibank. Corner of 64th and Madison. Box 305.

"Pinky raced into her big brother's room and asked him to

bring her cross-town. He wasn't in the mood, but she convinced him. Hard to say no to a girl as sweet as Pinky."

"Like me and Eli."

Laney nods. "Anyway, it was a short wait for the cross-town bus, and when its doors opened Pinky followed her brother onto the bus, waited as he swiped his MetroCard, and took a seat next to a little old lady with a small white dog. The city was beautiful, the park covered in snow, twinkling Christmas lights.

"The bus stopped right in front of the bank. Pinky said goodbye to the lady with the dog, thank you to the bus driver. She asked her brother to wait outside and made her way into the bank."

Laney checked her watch. "It really is getting late, Janey. Diane's going to honk any minute so I'm going to skip to the end of the story, okay, honey?"

"Okay, Mommy."

"Pinky sneaked into the room with all the safety deposit boxes."

"What is that?"

"You know, the room at the bank with those little boxes. You've been there—remember once you came with me to the bank and I put papers and some other things in a metal box?" Janey nods.

"Anyway, Pinky checked the numbers of every box against the numbers on her finger. When she found the match she stuck her pinky into the keyhole and, lo and behold, she turned her finger and the box opened."

Janey's eyes are wide.

"Inside the box was a velvet sack and inside the sack were the—"

"Stars!"

"How did you know that?" Laney asks, kissing Janey on the forehead.

"Why were they there?"

"Well, Blanche got nervous that Franz Finkelfarb would steal the glittering jewels, so when she left his store she went to the bank and locked them away in her safety deposit box. People like to think if you hide beauty it's safe.

"Anyway, Pinky grabbed the sack and stuffed it in her jacket pocket. She walked out the door of the bank, grabbed her brother's hand and asked him to take her home.

"'All done?' her brother asked.

"'Almost.'

"When they got home, Pinky hurried into her room, locking the door behind her. It was early still but the sky was already dark. Pinky raced over to the window, opened it, and began throwing the glittery stones into the dim sky. Now, I happened to be a little girl back then, and let me tell you. It was really something seeing those diamonds stick to the sky like that. Really something. And that's the end of the story."

"What about her finger, Mommy?"

"What about her finger—?"

"Did it get better?"

"Honey, that's the best part of the story. When Pinky woke up the next morning her finger was still the same but she didn't hate it anymore. In fact, as she looked at it, she thought it looked kind of cool. So she went into her mommy's room and asked her mommy to paint it."

Janey smiles.

"Guess what color."

"Red?"

"Nope."

"White?"

"Nope."

"Pink?"

"Yep." Laney kisses Janey on her forehead. "I have to go, honey."

"I have a wish," Janey says.

"What's your wish?"

"I can't tell it to you."

"Why?"

"Because then it won't come true."

"Who told you that?"

"I don't remember."

"Well, whoever told you that must not know about the 'Mommy clause.'"

"The Mommy clause?"

"You can always tell your mommy a wish."

"Good," the little girl says, throwing her arms around her mommy's shoulders. "I wish you would love me forever."

"You never have to worry about that, baby." Laney looks at Janey. The honey-colored hair that frames her face, her sloped nose, delicate ears. "I will always love you."

"Forever?"

"Forever and ever."

And then, as if on cue, Diane beeps her horn.

LANEY REACHES INTO HER BAG, GRABS

a pair of toenail scissors and begins sifting her fingers through her hair.

"What in the world are you doing?" Diane asks.

"Looking for dead ends." Laney says this matter-of-factly as if there's nothing unusual about being on the train, in a cocktail dress, with tiny gold scissors hanging out your mouth.

"Here's one." Laney gestures for Diane to come closer. "See that little white thing. That's a dead end." Laney snips it, puts the scissors back into her mouth and begins hunting again.

Diane plays along, "Who wants dead ends?" It's nearly, but not quite, perceptible, her fear.

Laney collects her dead ends in the palm of her hand. As the train pulls into the station she tosses the scissors back into her bag, opens her hand, and blows.

Fluff off a dandelion.

The station's buzzing.

"Gosh, Di, there's a lot of people here."

"Don't worry." Diane takes Laney by the hand. "I know exactly where we're going."

Laney's eyes drift. Newspapers, doughnuts, shoeshine boys. Flowers, pizza, cell-phone providers. People upon people push past.

Road-weary travelers, commuters, two suburban women in cocktail dresses.

No different than the ocean, they flood the station only to recede. Nameless, it is but a feeling, a tone. Low tide to high, continuous.

So it happens that Laney doesn't see him, not immediately. It takes her a second to focus in, but when she does she not only sees but hears it—him. The hell he's in. Rubber padding, sound proofing. Nothing can quiet. His visual exists as he does. Still and unformed.

They called them, growing up, kids like that: "short bussers." A guy Laney knew, seventh grade boyfriend, threw a stone at a short bus once. "Retards," he said, stepping off the curb. How annoying. That a short bus of all things should splatter dirty brown water on his new high-tops.

Now they are, the fortunate few, "Mainstreamers." The victory ramp: toilet with censor. This boy, perhaps, flushes his own. Music wafts through the air. The Rocky theme song. Stravinsky. "Freebird."

Head cocked, mouth open, saliva drips into the small blue cup his mother holds to his lips as they push forward. Through Grand Central and into the balmy evening air.

"He doesn't know anything different," Diane says before hailing a cab.

Doesn't he?

Solitary is confinement. He may not. But his mother knows. The struggle she has brought him.

"I wonder what Sheryl's going to look like," Diane says substituting noise for air.

"Pregnant," Laney says. Thrown, as she has been, by the retard at the train station her voice is flat, resigned.

But observe her as she is now. Dancing with a friend. Mere minutes. How she smiles. The costume irrelevant. So the clown dances. Arms in the air, a sequined tank. Laney appears as present as anyone else, everyone else at Sheryl's birthday party.

"I wish I could dance like you." Amy says, "I wish I could move like that."

"You could. All you have to do is feel the music."

Amy is trying, stepping side to side. "Every time I'm on the dance floor it's sixth grade trauma recurrence. I'm a foot taller than every boy. Girls are making fun of the way my feet turn out. 'Quack. Quack. Quack.'"

Laney takes the red Charms lollipop she's sucking on and breaks it between her two front teeth.

"There's nothing wrong with the way you dance, Amy. If there's anything wrong, it's that I'm still harboring a stripper fantasy."

"I could have been Senator." Bruce says from the side of the dance floor. Through the corner of her eye Laney sees him point at her, "But I married Laney." This to complete strangers.

That's not in Bruce's book is it? Nowhere in the bestselling *God and the Meaning of Insurance* is there a chapter on how best to utilize one's wife.

The excuses. The excuses people make for not becoming.

Does she react? Not our Laney. She didn't hear, did she? Fists up in the air like that. She spins round.

Never react.

"You okay, Lane?" Amy asks.

Never.

"Don't I look okay?"

Dinner is about to be served. Laney makes her way over to the table. There are drinks. More drinks. But Laney's being good. It's not worth it, not worth stumbling in this crowd.

"Hi, honey," Bruce says, pulling back the chair for her. "This is David and Carol Blackman."

Laney says hi, and takes her place at the table. She knows the routine so well she could nearly script it. Both men are basketball fanatics, think flat-screen televisions will come down, and the housing market's inflated.

Turns out this prospect's a garmento—has a hundred employees, a factory in Passaic. "I named the company, Knit 4 Pearl, after my wife." The word play continues, "Show 'em your ears, honey." The dumpling sitting next to him, his wife Pearl, pushes her hair back to reveal a giant set of—*tada*—Moby Pearls.

Hilarious.

But wait, what's this?

The Mrs. is piping up—with a gift yet—"You know, I've been thinking of writing a book. How did you do it, Bruce? Did you just sit down and type what you were thinking into a computer or did you like pay someone to help you?"

"It's sentence by sentence, Pearl. Anyone can do it. Call me at home. I'd be happy to help you." Bruce takes his card out of his wallet, a pen from his sport-coat pocket. He turns the card over, jots his phone number down, passes it across the table. There it goes, over the flower arrangements, straight down the center of the table. Pearl reaches—and it's a completion.

First down.

Now if you're the garmento you're sitting there thinking—my broker, what does he really do for me? Okay, he sells me insurance. Year in, year out. Bills quarterly. But this guy. Let's see:

1. Bruce is a family man.

2. He shares the same values.

3. He's happy to give you his home number.

4. He says he'll match your existing policy.

5. And, as if all that's not enough, the guy's got connections to the publishing world.

"What do you want to write a book about?" Laney asks.

"About how one event in your life can change everything."

"Really. How fascinating."

What a moron.

Like that's some fucking profound notion. Every fucking book is about that. That's what literature is. Anna meets Vronsky, Gatsby/Daisy, Humbert—

Laney reaches in her bag. "Excuse me." She gestures toward her cell phone. "I'm going to run and call the kids."

Laney makes her way through the club. Look at these people. Tight jaws, fake tans, trendy clothes. Here she is walking the straight and narrow to end up at some club in the city that hasn't been cool since she was in college.

How funny, she says to herself. You can be a New Yorker your whole life but once you move out, once you've got an E-ZPass with no maximum balance, you're as bridge and tunnel as the girl who grew up at Exit 14 off the Jersey Turnpike. Laney pushes through to the outside. The cool air feels good; she takes a breath, then another.

A cigarette. A cigarette would be good right now. As Laney's digging through her bag someone places a hand on her shoulder.

"The way you move out there on the dance floor. If I were Bruce I'd get you your own pole."

Laney turns. It's been a month since she's seen him.

"You look great," he says.

"Do I?"

Donny nods, "Like a million bucks."

"Thanks."

Silence.

White space.

"You have a light?"

"Of course."

Laney glances at her reflection in the club's window. She pushes her hair behind her ear, leans into the flame.

"You know, I was going to call you but then I thought I'd done enough, you know. Caused enough damage."

"It wasn't your fault, Donny—"

The lyrics of a Marianne Faithful song her mother used to play when Laney was a child plays in her head.

"You could have been any man, Donny."

"Is that right?"

"I didn't mean it like that. I just meant that I was looking for something—guess I'm still looking. Of course, it makes it harder that I don't know what I'm looking for. You were there, willing, and I thought maybe—maybe if I had, well that doesn't matter. Don't worry about it, Donny. You didn't drive me into rehab."

"I just want you to know I took your advice. Sheryl and I— we've been working on working it out."

"I saw."

"I didn't know. When that thing happened—you know—I want to make sure you know I had no idea Sheryl was pregnant."

This information is for whose benefit? Laney wonders. Did he want her to pat him on the back? *I know, buddy. You're no cheater. I seduced you. I made you fuck me in the ass.*

Absolution.

Asshole.

And from her, of all people. She's not a nun, not even a Catholic. Laney takes a drag, but it's more than that, it's not forgiveness he wants, not exactly. She looks Donny over, face to feet to face again. "I don't even know what you're talking about."

"Thanks." He takes a moment, then kisses her cheek. "I'm here for you, you know."

"Yep."

Donny makes his way back into the club. He even turns once to wave.

Eli answers on the first ring. "Hello?"

"How are you?"

"I'm okay, Mom."

"You sure?"

"I'm sure."

"That's good. Your sister still sleeping?"

"She's sleeping."

Across the street Laney watches an older man hold open a taxi door for a fake-looking blonde.

"Honey—"

"Yeah, Ma."

"You know I love you, honey."

"I know, Mom."

"Nah, not really. Not how much." Laney can hear him breathing.

"I want you to promise me, E. Promise me that you'll always remember that I love you. I really, really love you."

"I promise, Ma."

Laney takes her forefinger and wipes under each of her eyes.

"Ma, can I go now? I'm watching a game."

"Of course, honey. Of course you can go."

Back at the table Laney is full of personality. "I'm thinking of writing a book, too."

"Really," Bruce says, "on what?" Garmento and Dumpling wait with baited breath.

"On prostitution."

"Prostitution? What do you know about prostitution?"

"I don't. But when I was outside calling Eli I saw this old guy with this fake-looking blonde, half his age, and the thought came to me. Prostitution is the perfect example of the double standard. It's illegal to sell your body if you're poor but when you're rich—when you're rich it's perfectly acceptable. We just call it being a wife."

Bruce looks at her with hardened eyes.

Laney smiles, returns the stare.

Right back at you, baby.

Bruce turns away.

Scaredy cat.

Day after day. Insurance and the meaning of God. God and the meaning of Insurance.

You can't insure this, fuck face.

Laney thumps her head with the palm of her hand. *Can't wish this one away, Brucey.* The hospital, her falling apart. This isn't a game, a business transaction, or a bet for that matter.

Come on hot shot, ask me. Ask me what I was doing out there.

But he won't. Bruce won't say anything. Not a word.

Across the room Donny taps a spoon against a champagne glass. The guests quiet. "I'd like to make a toast to my beautiful wife."

Sheryl's already right up next to him, beaming.

"I know you guys are here to dance and have fun so I'm going to make this short. "Sher," he turns to address her, then says, "I just want you to know, Sher, when I drive away to work each morning and see you there waving to me, our son standing by your side, all I'm thinking is how fast can I get back to you.

"Thank you for putting up with me. I know I can be some pain in the ass sometimes. Happy birthday, honey."

AAAWWWW.

"And thank you for having my baby." Donny gives her belly a quick kiss, then turns and faces his audience, "Can you believe it? Second baby this woman's having for me."

Another mask. Laney wears hers well. See her smiling. She claps in synchronicity with the rest of the hands in the private party room.

Behind façade, she's safe. How much easier it is, to play the part ascribed:

"That's the nicest speech."
To give into the scenery:
"What pretty centerpieces."
To not fight anymore.

ILLUMINATED BY THE CITY'S LIGHT,

memory unfolds like a movie, scene by scene, on the glass of the passenger window.

Laney sees herself knocking. Two cups of coffee, one black, one sugar. She has a jelly doughnut in her bag, a pair of Bruce's shoes, a copy of *Siddhartha*. She looks younger. It becomes her: turquoise, denim, a billowing eyelet blouse.

Cowboy, his head tilted to the side, a cordless phone balanced between his shoulder and ear, opens the door, looks her up and down, gestures her toward the chair.

Laney sits down, waits for him to finish his conversation. "Great, Mrs. Feld, see you tomorrow at one."

"Tomorrow at one," Laney says after he hangs up the phone. "I'll be far far away by then."

Laney passes him the coffee and doughnut. "Thanks." He sits down next to her, opens the paper bag, brings the doughnut to his lips.

Watching it play out, Laney's certain that she was right to pretend. That it was first thing in the morning not twelve in the afternoon. That she hadn't already had breakfast. That she wasn't going home.

LANEY
I have until 2:30.

Cowboy lifts the doughnut to his mouth, chapped lips, rosy cheeks. He kisses her. First her mouth, then her shoulder. He stops, cups her face in his hands.

COWBOY
You want a lesson?

Laney turns away from the passenger window, glances at Bruce's face. They have twenty, thirty more minutes in the car together. She might reach for his hand, might say she's sorry. Because what she did tonight was wrong. She knows that. A good person doesn't humiliate her husband.

But then again a good person doesn't cheat, doesn't fuck around for sport. Good and bad, though, aren't mutually exclusive are they? At least she didn't, Laney rationalizes, at least she didn't pretend that what she had with John, with any of the men, was more than it was. Didn't fool herself into thinking she had any jurisdiction over their freedom. That the fucking had anything to do with love.

Those last few hours with John marked the conclusion. The remainder of life his own, no questions, no explanations. Laney insists she's okay with this arrangement, and she is. Most of the time.

Because they're fantasy.

Fine. Laney accepts that; Cowboy merely the physical manifestation of an alternate world. A world where one dead elk and a pile of dry wood is enough to sustain her through winter.

Still, it didn't *not* happen. Every shrink from here to Cleveland can try their best to mitigate the affair. But she didn't *not* feel what she's sure she felt.

Bruce slows for the toll. It's darker on the highway. Backlit, by fleeting headlights, the image is inconsistent. Still, both in and out of focus Laney sees herself.

LANEY

Bet you can't catch me.

There she is, the mare and her one. Nothing feels like that.

Rampant.

She is fast. She is free. She is capable.

Dr. Page insists she can learn to feel "fast" and "free" and "capable" here at home.

In a convertible?

There are other ways.

But in this movie John Wayne is right behind her, he won't let her get lost, won't let her fall.

That's his job.

Shouldn't it be everyone's?

Has Bruce let you fall?

Has he?

John pulls up alongside of her, slows.

COWBOY

Let's take a second.

Six years Laney'd been faithful. Same husband, same lips against lips, chest against chest. Yet that grass, that sky, that making love.

Laney looks again at her husband. Hands on steering wheel, eyes on road. There are, there's no denying, moments when Laney thinks she could leave him, move out west with the kids. She'd live in a small house in the shadow of a mountain. She could marry a cowboy, have his baby.

And then where?

Where what?

Where will you hide your disappointment?

Good ol' Dr. Page.

Motivators, if that's the right word, interest Laney. What motivates someone to do whatever. Not in the psychopharmacology sense. Sure, in her case it's partly chemical. Some combination of a mood disorder, impulse control, alcoholism. Still, whatever the diagnosis, whatever the fuck any of it means, there's no discounting she's a liar. A good liar at that.

When she's not being offended, not the subject of their conjecture, Laney's actually able to find some of it funny. The way people reduce a situation. Her mom's like that. Just the other day she said, "You know it's my fault you have an oral fixation." This referring to the lollipop Laney was turning in her cheek. "I should never have banned sugar from the house."

Laney wants to laugh. Mom should see this. Two horses tied to the tree that shades them. A man is on his back. A woman her knees. She's not shoving John's thick Irish dick into her mouth because it tastes like candy.

People, Laney understands, do what they do for lots of reasons, some complicated, some pretty straightforward. Laney's not sure what motivates her to do any of the things she does.

Sure, she's a little unhappy with Bruce. But not unhappy enough that she has the right to squeeze his balls.

It's mostly about shame, she's decided. Or more specifically, perhaps, her lack of it.

Either way, what Laney's starting to realize, that she didn't quite understand before, not fully anyway, is that there comes a time when you must ask yourself what in your life, if anything, is salvageable. And then, only after you've got that worked out, can you begin to ask yourself if it's worth salvaging anyway.

"I JUST DON'T GET IT. YOU EXCUSE

yourself from the table, say you're going to call home and check on the kids and then you come back babbling about how you're going to write a book on prostitution?"

Bruce signals for the exit. "I was just trying to close a deal. For all of us."

"I know."

"I don't think you do, Lane. I don't think you have any idea how hard I work to keep it all going. You act like it's all some big joke, like what I do for a living is beneath you somehow. I'm sorry, you know. I'm sorry I'm not some rich guy's son. I'm sorry I can't stay home and play with you all day long."

"I don't expect you to play with me all day."

"Well, if you don't, you're sure doing a hell of a good job making it look like you need a babysitter."

"I'm not fucked up, Bruce. I didn't drink or anything."

"Come with me."

"Come with you?"

"Yeah, I want you to come with me to the convention. They're giving me the presidential suite. A weekend at the Delano. What do you say? We need time together. Just us."

"That's tomorrow?"

"Plane doesn't leave until the late afternoon. I'm the keynote speaker. Come on, Lane. Newark to Miami. Back Sunday."

"The Lollipop Express!"

"The what?"

"The Lollipop Express. That's what my mom used to call it. All the kids with divorced parents, flying alone on Friday afternoons. Dragging their bags, homework assignments, baseball mitts."

"That's fucking sad."

"Not as sad as not going."

Bruce doesn't respond.

"You know once Rooster and I slept in the airport."

"Why?"

"We were going to visit my grandparents for the week. Mom was away somewhere with some guy she was dating. I think it was Bernie."

Bruce laughs.

"Bernie was actually very nice. An accountant."

"Of course he was."

"Don't be mean." Laney smiles, gives Bruce a playful tap on the shoulder.

"Rooster and I had made the trip before so it wasn't a big deal or anything but our flight got canceled, snow or something so we spent the night."

"Why didn't your mom come and get you?"

"Rooster couldn't reach her. No cells back then, remember?"

"So what did you do?"

"We ate hotdogs."

Bruce is upset by this. "I hate your fucking parents."

"No," Laney laughs, "I mean you can hate them but not for that."

"You must have been scared."

"I don't think so, not really. I remember looking through the window at all the grounded planes, eating my hotdog. I was with Rooster, so, no. I don't think I was scared.

"I remember him asking me, if I could go anywhere in the world, where would I want to go?"

"Where did he want to go?"

"I don't know, somewhere out west. Wherever the Super Bowl was that year."

"And where did you want to go?"

"I didn't want to go anywhere really. And when I told Rooster that, he got all bent out of shape. Told me that everyone wanted to go somewhere. But where I wanted to go he couldn't take me so what was the point of talking about it." Bruce slows at an intersection. Looks right, left—

"What I remember most is waking up that morning, I remember it like yesterday. Waking up and feeling invisible, like me and Rooster weren't even there. No one seemed to notice us camped out in the corner waiting for our flight. I didn't realize it then, but looking back it was the first time I understood how little my existence mattered. You know what I mean, Bruce, how when you're a kid you think the whole world somehow revolves around you. I never thought about when that changed for me. But it started then. There we were, two kids, alone at the airport—no one asked us if we were okay or needed anything and we didn't. We were perfectly fine. But for some reason I remember thinking—like it suddenly occurred to me, that it didn't matter if we lived or died. It's not that no one cared about us, I knew my mom would be upset when she found out what happened and my grandparents were probably all worried. Rooster and I were loved, but we were insignificant. The airport was crowded with people just like us, people trying to get to some place other than where they were. And it would always be like that. The world has an endless supply of people."

"So you became an existentialist in Newark Airport."

"I guess so."

Bruce signals, turns onto their street. "Where did you want

to go?" he asks. "Cause I know you and you definitely wanted to go somewhere."

"You're going to laugh."

"When have I ever laughed at you?"

"Well, I wanted to go back, to when my dad lived with us. I wanted to find him in the kitchen mopping the floor with a dish towel beneath his feet."

"It's what Springsteen always talks about. Wanting to go back, to make it right."

"Yeah. Well, that's what I wanted. I wanted to go home."

Bruce pulls into their driveway. "You're home now," he says, his voice sincere, even hopeful.

"I guess I am."

"So will you come?"

Laney looks at her house. "Who'll watch the kids?"

"My parents—"

"And what about Eli? I can't keep coming and going. He's a mess as it is."

"Happy parents make happy kids."

"I don't know, Bruce. I hate Florida."

Bruce turns off the engine, looks at her. "You hate your father, Lane. You don't hate Florida."

TODAY—

- –drop-off
- –Market
- –manicure, pedicure, wax
- –drycleaners
- –Dr. Page @1:00
- –pick-up
- –do something with the kids—doughnuts?
- –pack
- –airport
- –florida

At drop-off, Mrs. Zeldis, Eli's first grade teacher, gestures for Laney to take a seat at the small kids' table just outside the door.

"I wanted to speak to you alone. Don't worry. It's not a big deal, but Eli is calling out too much."

"Calling out?"

"Interrupting—asking questions that he knows the answers to. I told him I'd love to answer all his questions but I have twenty-two other kids I have to teach. So anyway, if it's okay with you I'm thinking of giving him chips to hold."

Laney doesn't get it. "Chips?"

"I'll give him a certain number of chips every morning; each time he asks a question I'll take a chip and when he uses them up he uses them up. That's it. No more questions for the rest of the day."

"I see," Laney says.

"It's the way I like to teach kids like Eli."

Kids like Eli?

If depression is darkness, then the child of depression grows up living in the shadow of that darkness. Laney knows this from her own childhood. What we inherit—indiscriminate.

"Is he exhibiting compulsive behavior at home? I'm not sure you've seen him do it, but there's this thing he does with his eyes."

Just this morning. A bowl of Lucky Charms.

"Stop doing that, Eli."

"I can't control it, Dad."

"What do you mean?"

"My eyes, Dad. I can't control this—" Eli blinked again.

How to respond?

Laney chose silence.

Not Bruce. "Yes you can, son. You just have to fight the urge."

Bruce didn't get it, doesn't. He could pick every marshmallow out of that damn box. Fill Eli's cereal bowl with green clovers and blue diamonds.

She could learn the names of the Knicks' starting lineup. Memorize the move of every professional wrestler. They could cuddle him in the groove of their arms before bed, tell him they love him, believe in him. Insist he can be anything he wants to be. None of it will matter; Eli is wired to implode.

"No. I haven't seen that." This a lie. Laney lied.

Mrs. Zeldis rests the palm of her hand on Laney's shoulder. "It's all going to be okay."

The gesture reminds Laney of the time her mother patted Caroline Kennedy on the shoulder. "Caroline was walking right at me so I reached out, put my hand on her shoulder and said, 'I'm sorry.' And to think she pushed me away—"

"You must have scared her, Ma."

"Please. We were on Madison Avenue."

"Her brother just died."

"And that's exactly my point. I wanted her to know I was sorry."

It's funny, Laney thinks, how we project the manifestations of our fear by assuming another's pain, try to. Not only had Eileen never met Caroline Kennedy, Eileen's a Republican.

"Thank you," Laney says to Mrs. Zeldis, her voice contrite, her smile mastered.

In truth, Laney is besieged with regret. The wicked, taunting little laugh that haunts her is back, roaring in and out her head. Insisting that she finally accept she's not good enough. Not for the kind of happiness she's after.

Pig.

TODAY—

—drop-off
That's over, thank God.
—Market
Can phone in.
—manicure, pedicure, wax
Good.
—drycleaners
Pick up Monday.
—Dr. Page @1:00
Dr. Page, Dr. Page, Dr. Page.

Laney drives.

Scarlet polish on fingers and feet. Brazilian, low pile. *And then you die.*

Grocery store: orange juice, milk, yogurt, bananas, and a bag of marshmallows. *And then you die.*

Dry cleaners: one suit, two shirts, and a pair of slacks. Shirts should be folded—not hung. *And then you die.*

This voice, Laney understands, is something outside herself. Impulse, fantasy, she has names for it now, medical terms. It is, whatever she chooses to call it on a particular day, autonomous in thought. A parallel structure with a velocity all its own.

There are rules. She gets that. That there are rules to follow.

Things she can do to mitigate the degree of doubt. Like keeping this list. Every hour is scheduled, no idle time to daydream, fixate, get into trouble.

Laney tucks today's list into her bag. She's doing everything she can. She's not drinking, not smoking, not fucking people she's not supposed to be fucking. Still, the voice is not silenced. No matter what she accomplishes it answers her.

Sober.

A hot dog.

A baseball game.

Easing mustard out a tinfoil wrapper.

The evening sky blue.

The air cool.

Your boy.

Your husband.

Overtime.

A lifetime.

And then you die.

Nothing has any meaning, because, and this is how every sentence ends for her... *and then you die.*

The medicine makes her feel bloated. Most noticeably in the brain. Her head, she's come to accept as "other"—which leads her to wonder who owns it. Who is the actual proprietor of her brain?

Her body is her own. That she's certain of. Even her tits. Paid for and enjoyed, although not exclusively, by the very man who insisted she didn't need them. Who, in fact, argued against them. "They won't feel real," he said.

Yet, Laney's tits have become a fan favorite. How easy it was for Bruce, and herself for that matter, to acclimate to foreign matter. But then we are built this way. The resiliency of the human spirit is predicated on this very expectation. The body will always adapt providing the mind serves as alibi.

Laney reaches for her Diet Coke. Slow. All her actions seem

slow. A pill to pause. No. There's a better word for it. A pill to neuter. That's how it feels sometimes. As if she's being neutered. To be successfully neutered. *And then you die.*

But that's not Laney. Not the core of herself. The her that wants to mother her kids, wife her husband. This, the constant reminder of the futility in life, the pain, the utter disconnect, is the disease talking. *Fists in the air.*

What will happen, she wonders, when cancer has a cure? Where will those pesky cancer cells attack? What will they feed on without death as their definition of worth?

Understandably things seem slower. Laney's fine with this. That's what the medicine does. It slows things down. And yet she is somehow agitated. Dry in the mouth, her voice reverberates back at her. *And then you die.*

"Stop." As if by sheer will she will defy logic and suck the words back inside herself. Better there, inside her body where she can contain it.

Laney pulls into the spot reserved for outpatients. What's she going to talk about today? She can complain about the dry mouth. How's that? That's a new one. Evening sweats. The weight she's gained. How much time will that eat up?

Not enough.

Something. She better come up with something because the one thing she's not going to do today is talk about her father. So he left. So the fuck what?

And she did too much blow. Popped too many Xanax. It's old news already. Laney's feeling, if not to a large extent, certainly to a noticeable extent, better. To talk, to complain about any of it makes her feel like one of those women who sit around whining about the inconvenience of their $85,000 kitchen renovation.

People are starving, honey.

There is Eli, though. She needs to talk to Dr. Page about Eli. But how? How's she going to utter the words? How's she going to explain to Dr. Page what it feels like to know that Eli will never grow into the man he could have, would have grown into if he had a different mother. A mother with hand-eye coordination, speed—a mother who knew how to do more than cripple.

Paper and crayons.

In the office waiting room there's a bowl of crayons and a pad of unlined white paper. Laney sits on the carpet, tucks her knees under the coffee table. She pulls a crayon from the bowl, a sheet of paper from the pad. She looks at his door, checks her watch. She takes a breath and then, just as the child preceding her did, she begins to draw.

"SO ELI'S BORN AND MY IN-LAWS ASK

me if they can have his bris at their apartment. I don't really like the idea too much but okay. It's their first grandson. I get it. So I say, 'Sure. No problem. Just the family though.' They assure me that it will only be the family and perhaps, if I don't mind, one or two of their closest friends.

"That seemed reasonable. But sure enough, when I walk in the doors there were like eighty people on line at a buffet. There was enough nova there to pay for Eli's college education."

Dr. Page chuckles.

"So anyway, the mohel comes and does his business and I actually start to exhale. That's over—made it through—done. But then, Harlene Brody, my mother-in-law's best friend, asks me where I'm planning to bury Eli's tip."

"The tip?"

"That's exactly what I said, 'The tip?'"

"And she says, 'The foreskin. It's bad luck, you know, if you don't bury it in dirt.'

"Well, it was as if a wall fell on me. I ran into the kitchen, checked the trash—empty. I rang for the elevator. I was absolutely apoplectic. I raced down to the basement, begged the porter to help me, and spent the next half-hour hunting through the building's garbage for Eli's tip.

"After about twenty minutes I locate our garbage. As

I'm digging through soggy bagels, picked-at rugelah, pulpy half-empty glasses of orange juice—frantic, a complete crazy person—I spot a Ziploc with bloody gauze in it. I rejoice. I shout to the poor guy helping me. 'It's in here. It's in here.' I open the bag, stick my hand in, unwrap every piece of tissue and gauze—but nothing. No tip."

Laney takes a breath.

"I thought for sure that I had ruined Eli's life, eight days old and his chance for happiness denied. So I thank the guy helping me, he must have thought I was out of my mind, which I guess I was, and took the elevator back up to my in-law's apartment. I found Bruce in the den.

"'Where've you been, honey?'

"'Bruce, do you have the mohel's phone number?' I was hysterical.

"'Why? What's wrong?'

"'The tip. I don't know where he put the tip and Harlene told me that if he didn't bury it in dirt it's very bad luck for Eli.'

"Bruce was baffled, but I didn't have time to dilly-dally and explain. I walked around his chair, picked up the phone, and paged the guy. A few minutes later the mohel calls back from his cell, 'Something wrong?'

"I say, 'So sorry to bother you but my mother-in-law's friend just told me that if I didn't bury Eli's tip in dirt it was bad luck.'

"'Tip?'

"'Foreskin.'

"'Oh, the foreskin. Don't worry about it. I buried it in a pot on 61st and Madison. Right in front of Barney's.'"

Laney, is quiet. "Anyway—"

Outside Dr. Page's window the breeze rustles through what's left of the autumn leaves. There's only so long he'll let her stall. Laney looks at her doctor. "Eli's getting worse. His teacher pulled me aside this morning and told me he's shouting out in class and she asked me about his twitching. If I noticed it, the way he repeatedly blinks his eyes, or any other change in his behavior."

"What did you tell her?"

"I told her no. That he seemed perfectly fine at home."

"Why did you lie?"

"It just seemed like the better thing to do."

"I told you though, Eli's ticking has nothing to do with your disorder."

"What is my 'disorder'?"

"I'm not sure yet."

"Then how can you be sure that he—?"

"Because whatever conditions you have, they aren't uniformly transmitted."

"What does that even mean?"

"It means that while there's a genetic component it's not the only prerequisite. Environment plays a big part in it."

"It doesn't matter, Dr. Page."

"What doesn't matter?"

She looks up. "I'm Eli's mother." Tears trickle down her cheeks, scratching her face like small hardened stones.

"You know last night, after Bruce and I got back from the city, I went into each of the kids' rooms to check on them like I always do. I sat down on the edge of Eli's bed. Watched him breathe in, then out. And I thought to myself, he'll never know. Neither of them will ever know how hard I tried not to hurt them."

THE AIRPORT IS CROWDED, EVEN

midweek, the supply of people endless. One by one, pimply-faced, overweight characters come and go, dragging their cameras, their kids, fighting to get upgraded to first class. A man waits for his daughter. A wife for her husband.

The college student returns for a weekend visit: backpack, hangover, newly minted coffee drinker. His mother, presently outside circling Baggage, has been preparing all week. Ironed sheets, homemade lasagna, iced sugar cookies.

A blonde-haired woman with bright red lips and a coordinated red rolling bag walks past. Squeals as she opens her arms: one, two, three grandchildren! There is, Laney thinks as she waits on line, innocence to these airport scenes. Funny, of all places for emotion to be real.

But is it?

Nah. The cynical side of Laney, the smarter side, intervenes. *Sure, I'll miss you, baby.*

See that guy playing it out with the tight, long embrace. The one at the Northwest counter. There he goes, checking the time as he grips his wife by the waist. Twenty more minutes till take off.

Goddamn is he keyed up. Hands in and out of pockets, legs shuffling from side to side. Convention blavention! In six hours, Tahoe. Good ol' Suzy'll be riding him bareback. Yahoo! You go, cowgirl.

"I think this used to be the Eastern Airlines terminal."

Bruce is preoccupied, there's a long wait at security and although they're an hour early he's worried about missing the plane. He checks his watch.

"Really?"

"The airport looks exactly the same. I mean the terminal's been renovated—"

"And there's no more Eastern Airlines—"

"Yep, no more Eastern Airlines. But when we walked in here, Bruce, gosh, so many memories came rushing into my head. The smell of this place, they must use the same cleaning solution they did back then."

Bruce smiles at her. "Is this the first time we've flown Newark instead of LaGuardia?"

"I guess so." Laney feels detached. It's as if the child she was, the girl who spent weekends meandering around this terminal, is her own entity. Perhaps whatever it is that Laney lost can finally be found.

"Next." The man behind the counter is summoning them.

"Come, hon," Bruce says.

Laney follows her husband's lead, rests her bag on the table, lifts her arms. The security guard, a fat black woman brandishing a handheld device, passes it along Laney's side. A wand waving at reality. If only it were that easy, to pinpoint the ugly, discard it.

What do they look like, she and Bruce? Husband and wife going where? Do they look like they have two kids at home? Do they look happy?

"Take your shoes off, miss."

"My shoes?" Laney bends over, places her boots in the plastic bin and waits.

"You're okay."

Laney wants to make a joke, "Bzzz. How wrong you are, missy." But she doesn't. Instead, she gathers her things and walks with Bruce over to the newsstand.

"Check this out." Bruce opens the *Journal* and points to a full-page ad for his book. Laney can't believe it. "This must have cost them a fortune." Bruce smiles, his cell rings, "Meet me outside." He motions for Laney to pay and walks into the terminal. Laney grabs an *Elle Décor* and *People*, a Diet Coke, strawberry Balance bar.

"But Mom said I could." At the register a brother is arguing with his sister over a bag of M&M's. The boy is just around Eli's age, the sister older, twelve maybe. "Mom said I could buy two things."

"It's not that I don't want you to have both of them, Sam, I just need to make sure we have enough money." The boy's shoulders collapse.

Bruce folds his phone, walks back into the store. "What's taking so long?" Laney stands on her toes and whispers in his ear, "Nothing changes." She points in the direction of the children.

This shuttling of children, the by-product of an aborted love. Happiness an afterthought, their happiness. She feels for the pin above her lapel: Laney Forrester, 333 West End Avenue. 212-467-2233.

"I don't think so," Bruce says, "but if it'll make you feel better, buy the kid his candy. In fact," Bruce checks his watch, "twenty minutes until boarding. You have my permission to stand here and buy every kid you feel sorry for a candy bar."

He smiles, puts his arm around her shoulder, "You're a sweet person, Lane."

Bruce is only being playful; still it isn't something to make light of. As a kid, to have a bag full of candy would have made Laney feel—nothing. That's the truth. The pain doesn't go away. Not even with an endless supply of chocolate bars.

A man, knapsack, tennis racquet, violet rolling bag, has entered this picture. "What's up, guys?"

"Dad, I want a bag of M&M's and Anna says I can't have both things."

"I just said we had to make sure I had enough money."

"I have cash, Brian." Suddenly a woman appears. She reaches into her bag, a canvas tote, passes her husband a twenty.

"See, beauty"—Bruce wraps his arm around Laney's waist, squeezes her close—"those two are okay. They have parents and everything."

These are the moments that continue to haunt. In and out the distance of Laney's mind, memory travels, compressing what was with what is, confusing her.

On the plane a flight attendant offers them drinks.

"No, thank you." Laney has her Diet Coke.

"A Diet Coke would be great." Bruce takes his soda, puts it on the armrest between them. "Two hours, forty-three minutes."

Now the flight attendant is congratulating the couple across the aisle. "Honeymoon, how wonderful."

Drinks poured. More conversation.

"Your cruise departs Sunday. How perfect. That gives you two whole days to recuperate from the wedding."

Laney lifts the soda can to her mouth. Away, on the far side of a punctured sky, miles of buffet await them. Vats of Piña Coladas, fifteen-dollar jars of Coppertone, hope.

Laney swallows.

She was that girl.

"Are you going to call him?" Bruce asks.

"Who?"

"Your dad."

"No. Why would I do that?"

"Maybe it's just time."

"Time for what?"

"Time to let go of the anger."

"But I'm not angry."

"Of course you are."

PAM SINGER IS A THIRTY-SOMETHING

blonde from Potomac. She is married to an underwriter named Steven. Together, they have three kids, two sons, Max and Deno, ages five and seven respectively and an eighteen-year-old daughter. The daughter, a nameless remnant from Steven's first marriage, is enjoying her sophomore year at University of Maryland. Max and Deno are, at present, in the competent hands of Pam's mother and Filipino nanny.

They live, the Singer family, in a newly constructed, "Turn of *this* century home."

Ah, the drama of the clever housewife, the wasted potential—

"It's in a development which is nice for the kids. There's a golf course, a snack-shack. It's quite cute. Of course, I would have preferred my bedroom to have a view of seventeen, but Steven didn't think it was worth—"

"—Course property is overrated. All those fertilizers seeping into your drinking water."

Please, Pam, volunteer more. Because Laney is bored out of her fucking mind here. Politics, the imminent threat of terrorism, nipple piercing. Just no more insurance talk. No more "term" versus "whole life."

You want to "bump up" the value on your policy—bump up the fucking value. The bottom line about life insurance is, it only pays once. Bruce should add that to his book. Next printing. And while he's at it, he should mention that if you slit your wrists you might miss out on the death benefit.

"My lease is up in a year and then I'm going to get a hybrid."

"I drive an SUV too," Laney says. "Sometimes I feel guilty but Bruce says it's safer—he studies the actuarial charts."

"Safe? It's not safer for your kids to have polluted air to breathe. Do you know that the number of children diagnosed with asthma is rising at a rate of—" Pam does her part: a spring luncheon at the Four Seasons, "I'm on a mission to help save the rainforest. You should come."

"What a nice invitation."

What else? What else you doing with your life, Pammy?

Pam used to work at Williams-Sonoma, which is where she met Steven. "He was buying a spatula." Now she's a stay-at-home mom "searching for meaning."

All this information has been amassed in a matter of minutes by Laney, who, after having finished her first glass of wine (*"It's only wine," she told Bruce as he eyeballed her drink*) has returned to the bar for seconds. "I just love your gown," Pam says as they make their way back to the ballroom. "I was never a minimalist. Fuck, Prada. That's a dress. Lilac. Great choice, lilac. You know, when I saw you earlier today in the lobby—"

"The lobby?" Laney lifts her lips from the edge of her glass.

"You were in the gift shop buying lollipops."

Laney nods, having placed herself. Late afternoon, on the way to the beauty salon.

"When I saw you I just knew we'd be friends."

"How did you know?"

"You in those Birkenstocks and jean shorts, a bandana around your head, enough lollipops for an entire kindergarten class. Girl after my own heart. But I prefer bubble-gum."

With this Laney lets out a long, exhaustive yawn.

"Am I boring you?"

"Oh my goodness, not at all. I just hardly slept last night, hard time leaving the kids and Bruce has this speech to make and—you were telling me about the book you're working on."

"Not a book. I'm not a writer like your husband. I mean please, who knows where it will go. I'm just journaling. It's part of this whole program I'm doing to center myself. My Yogi—"

"You have a Yogi?"

"Don't you?"

Laney shrugs her shoulders. "I have a trainer and a shrink but no Yogi."

"Well, Joey says—"

"Joey?"

"Joey Abruzzi. And stop with your laughing. He went to Divinity School at Harvard and he spent like, I don't know, ten years studying in Tibet with a disciple of the Dalai Lama. His whole thing is basically to go back to the beginning. To the moment you're released from the womb and try to reclaim that person. That spirit—the soul that was stolen from you."

"What do you mean by stolen?"

"In the sense that all our spirits are. All of us are born pure. It's the world that corrupts us. Toxic chemicals, toxic thoughts. He starts you with a thirty-day cleansing where you only drink liquids. Whole foods are introduced, but not all at once. I'm like a baby. One new food group at a time. Last week carrots, this week avocado.

"Anyway, he has you do the same with knowledge. Same thirty days. No television, no newspapers. 'Emptying,' he calls it. Dumping all non-essential information. The waste in your brain."

"I could do without the TV and newspapers but music—"

"You'd be surprised. I actually feel much better now that I'm not watching 'Entertainment Tonight.' I can't compete with those young girls. And there's music, Joey sells these CDs of Tibetan hymns."

Pam opens a Ziploc filled with pills and looks at Laney. "You just can't listen to pop or rock, and absolutely no talk radio."

"What are those?"

"Joey has me taking all sorts of vitamins, food supplements. I take about eighteen a day. Vitamin C as an antioxidant. An E, a multi-carotene, folic acid. B-6 for my hair, mushroom compounds for my immune system, calcium."

"That looks like a Xanax," Laney says, eyeing the little white pill.

"Joey says Xanax is absolutely necessary, that it's a bridging drug. Helps to straddle the abyss. Between what was and what will be."

"Can I have one?" Laney asks. "Left my supply at home."

"Sure, take as many as you want. I can't imagine how I'd get through this weekend without mine. All these wives keeping tabs on their husbands' bottom lines. Control was a big hurdle for me. Learning to accept that I have no control over any of it: Steven making his numbers, screwing his assistant, getting a brain tumor."

Laney nods her head, sipping slowly from her Rum and Coke.

"If Osama Bin Laden decides to have one of his cronies blow up The Mall of America, I have absolutely no control. Joey and I have worked really hard on this. He says all I can do is look for what's missing inside myself."

Laney wants to ask Pam Singer if she's fucked Guru Joey yet or has he merely gone down on her. Munching at the edge of her abyss as it were.

"So you want to know today's thought?" Pam asks.

"Want to tell me it?" The familiar haze has begun to set in, and Laney feels better, better than she has in quite some time. Safe.

"Well, I woke up early this morning and I went out to the beach, the sun was rising and I felt at peace. Real peace, you know. I was sitting there and I thought, stop being so hard on yourself, Pam. And that's when it occurred to me: To exist is to be. You know what I mean. To merely exist—"

"That's good," Laney says, humoring herself.

"To tell you the truth," Pam continues, "I didn't actually come up with that. It's one of Joey's mantras. But out there on the beach this morning. Well for the first time I got it—as long as you continue to breathe you are in it, you know?"

"I sure do," Laney says, watching the tables fill. "As long as you breathe you are part of the game."

"I think it's about to start," Pam says, offering Laney a handful of Xanax. "This should get you through the rest of the weekend."

"Thanks," Laney says, tucking the pills in the pocket of her beaded evening bag.

"Underwriters, fellow policy holders, ladies and gentleman. I'm proud to introduce to you tonight's speaker. Bruce Brooks has been in the insurance business for the past fifteen years. He is a husband and father and last but not least, the author of the bestselling book, *God and the Meaning of Insurance*."

Laney pulls at Pam's dress, motioning her to bend down. "There's one thing I want to know," Laney whispers into her new friend's ear. "To be what?"

Pam looks bewildered.

"Ask that guru of yours. Tell him you met this woman at the convention and she wants to know—she wants to know what the fuck you're supposed to be, what you are—when you're busy existing. Make sure you get back to me when you figure that part out."

And with this, Laney turns her attention to the stage. She straightens her back, smiles as her husband makes his way from the dais to the podium and continues clapping even after the rest of the applause has quieted.

"MORNING, BABE."

"You were great last night," Laney says, looking at him. Bruce has sweet eyes, a soft but sturdy chest.

"That's cause you were here."

"Please."

"Really, it's true. When I looked into the audience I thought somewhere out there is my pretty wife."

"I think you were thinking somewhere out there is a guy in need of some heavy-duty life insurance."

"You're so cynical."

Laney lowers her voice, imitating her husband, "Drive a wedge between man and his fears and he'll pay nearly anything to—"

"Are you mocking me, miss look-at-my-new-diamond-wedding-band?"

Laney stretches her arms above her head, admires the white row of diamonds glistening in the early morning light. Who would have thought that Bruce, a bookie when she met him, would turn out to be the author of a bestselling book, a keynote speaker at a national convention, a respected man.

"I just can't believe it, Bruce. Look at what you've done with your life."

Bruce kisses her forehead. "I wouldn't have any of it without you, Lane." And with that, he's at the window raising the shade.

"Man, what a gorgeous day. I better go down to the pool, get our chaise situation all worked out. Tip the cabana boy. Why don't you get dressed and meet me in the dining room. We'll have brunch. Tee off isn't until 12."

Laney sits, her back pressed against the white leather headboard. "Why don't we fuck first?"

It is only here, perhaps, that she has the power to keep him. But for how long? Laney hardens him with her mouth, then rolls over on all fours, eager to service. Bedded down by his weight she is but a fantasy. Forward, her face shadowed by a veil of long hair, she moves—sways even. Hers the easy rhythm of the imposter.

After, Bruce, in a newly purchased ensemble: banana-colored polo shirt, limegreen trousers, grins the grin of the satiated man. "I'll be back by seven." He checks his pockets, "Phone, wallet—"

"Have a good time," Laney says, the door closing behind him.

Her pussy still works, which is an important thing, to know that it works, winking at her from down below. It is a testament to her survival. Well groomed, well trained in divisiveness. It lies about its age, its ownership.

"Don't worry," Cowboy mumbled, his mouth tangled in her wire. His palms eased her thighs, "I won't hurt you."

Worry? It didn't occur to Laney to worry back then. She was enjoying herself. The young man's head between her legs. She tugged at his sandy hair, unbridled.

And now?

Laney rolls on her side, glances at the clock, 11:45.

Now she worries. Not about getting caught as much as betrayal. Her unrelenting desire to betray. She doesn't taste bad yet, surely not any worse than her husband does. She feels a little sorry, but no more than a little. Dirty cock discharging. Damn Bruce, leaving her to drift, without purpose, around this fucking hotel.

There's the pool. She can go out to the pool and catch some

sun or lie in bed all day and read her book. The hotel has a spa. Maybe she should check that out, schedule a facial, a massage.

Or.

She focuses on the phone.

Maybe.

Dr. Page says demons are smaller when they are behind you.

Laney opens her evening bag, takes a Xanax from the zipper compartment, swallows. She reaches for the phone, dials.

"City and State?"

"Roger Forrester"

"City and state?"

Fucking computers.

"Boca Raton, Florida. Roger Forrester."

"There's no Roger Forrester in Boca but we have one in Hollywood."

As Laney jots down the number, a lifetime of questions begin to race through her mind. Does he have a favorite television show, a favorite cookie, a favorite color? What's he do for a living now? Does he have a girlfriend? Is he happy?

But as the phone rings there is only one. After Laney says hello, after she explains where she is and invites him to lunch she'll ask him.

Nicely. No anger.

She needs it explained to her again, one last time, why it was he left.

And when he's through explaining his side of the story, because there's always two sides to a story, three as they say, she'll tell him how much she missed him, how much she still misses him.

I wish you could have known me then. I was such a good girl.

The phone is answered on the second ring by the voice of a young child. "Hello?"

"Oh, I'm sorry," Laney says, "I must have the wrong number."

"Who's on the phone, Daisy?" But it's not the wrong number. Even in the background his voice—

"No one, Daddy."

Laney feels herself being passed from daughter to father. "Hello?"

A really good little girl.

"Hello?"

Laney gathers herself, "Does she look like me?"

"Who is this?"

"Do you sing her a lullaby before bed?"

"Laney?"

Laney doesn't answer. She carries the phone over to the dresser, takes a vodka from the mini-bar.

"I'm in Florida, Dad."

"For how long?"

"Until tomorrow. Bruce has a convention."

"I read his book. Really interesting."

"Yeah."

"He's absolutely right. People try to manage their fears by securing them."

"Is that what you did?"

"Laney, tell me where you're staying and I'll come get you."

It was stupid. This is what Laney tells herself as she makes her way into the bathroom. The whole idea, calling her father out of the blue like that was plain stupid. And then jumping at the chance to see him. What good could possibly come from this?

"And here's..." drum roll, spaghetti straps, twirl. *Please!* Laney needs that little ferret-face virgin—*sister. That's what the voice on the other end of the phone is, it's the sound of her sister.* Laney needs that saccharinley sweet ferret-faced virgin sister of hers in her life like she needs a hole in the head. *Who's on the phone, Daisy? No one, Daddy.*

Knees against chest, two pretty feet pressed into a pale

marble floor, Laney waits for the tub to fill. Her left thigh, she notices, bulges where it should be smooth. Too much oatmeal for breakfast.

She stands, moves to the toilet, leans over, sticks her fingers down her throat, and pulls. Finished, she wipes her eyes, brushes her teeth, then slowly steps into the bath.

No. Going to his house is the right thing to do. He can't get away with this. She'll be like the Trojan horse. He'll open his front door willingly. Once inside, she'll out him. Tell little sister the story... *when I woke up in the morning he was gone*.

And the wife, too. Laney will help with the dishes, a sudsy kitchen sink. "So Barb, how do you handle Dad's drinking?"

Even if Barb's steeped in denial, all "He hasn't had a drink for..." and little sister gets hysterical, "My daddy would never..." Laney will have succeeded. She will have planted the fear. They'll tell themselves that they're different, that he's different, but the residue of Laney's comments will fester.

Laney lowers her head into the warm bath water. She feels slightly dizzy and even a little scared but for the first time in a long time she knows what she wants.

Laney wants to be a flower.

No, Laney wants to be the butterfly on the flower, translucent, graceful. She wants to go out into the world and steady what's left of herself on the tip of a butter-colored petal. She's bound to be captured, just as her back arches, her wings wave, stars push through the specific evening's sky.

But that one second, she imagines.

BLOCK BY BLOCK, THE BOY FRAMES

the building. It will be, he insists, taller than the Twin Towers. His mother watches, wondering how, since he knows what can happen, he continues to build.

Block by block.

The base is not large enough to support the structure's height and she tells him this. But if he makes it bigger he might run out of blocks before the building is tall enough. And he wants a tall building. He has envisioned a tall building.

Even if it exists for just an instant before collapsing. A fraction of a second. It will have existed. The boy will be able to boast—to his brother, his kindergarten friends, his teacher. "When I was in Florida, I built a building so tall that it toppled over on itself." This is both frightening and exhilarating, frighteningly exhilarating to the boy. To build what cannot be sustained.

Moving through the lobby, Laney registers the scene, thinks of her own son. He's not a builder of buildings though. Not like some kids. Some kids, like this kid, can spend hours playing with blocks. Not Eli. He's never been interested in the geometry of the world.

For Eli, life has always been binary. By the time he was this boy's age, he had divided the world into good and evil. You were either Batman or the Joker. He was Batman.

Now, at eight, and a Yankee fan, it's a bit more complicated.

The thought of her son makes Laney smile and smiling reminds her of the segment she saw this morning on a local Florida news station. Some guy had two palm trees flatbedded up north to his house in Sheepshead Bay. It was his twenty-fifth wedding anniversary and he wanted to do something special for his wife. "Why not take her on vacation to Florida?" the reporter asked. "Wouldn't that have been easier?"

The man, a fifty-something guy with a thinning head of hair, put his arm over his wife's shoulder. In a backyard framed by yellowing oaks and orange maples they swayed on a hammock suspended between deep green palms. "Anyone can go to Florida."

Anyone can go…

Laney passes through the hotel doors and continues toward the taxi that will take her to her father's home. It has been years now, over twenty-five since he left. Long enough for the couple on television to raise a family, pay down a mortgage, even flatbed two palm trees over a thousand miles to their home. Long enough for Laney to accept that her dad's leaving was by choice.

"Excuse me, sir, do you mind if I smoke?"

"Not a problem," the taxi driver answers. There is no effort to make eye contact. He doesn't care that Laney's good-looking, doesn't care about fucking her—her name, her face, her story is meaningless to him. His only obligation is to get her from point A to point B and for that he'll be compensated. Theirs is an honest exchange.

Which is how it's going to be for now on. No more lies. Laney's going to go over there and expose her father for what he is. Put an end to the unfairness. Why should her dad get to start over—to redo—to correct the mistakes he made the first time round when she can't.

He can take his new daughter to ball games, share popcorn at the movies—he can coach her soccer team. Laney's dad, their dad, can be anything he wants to be if she lets him.

But not Laney. She can be a mother and a wife but she can never be a little girl again. Never know love free of fear.

Laney reminds herself of her objective. "Trojan horse," she says quietly. "I'm the Trojan horse."

It is with this in mind that she finds the inner strength to press the doorbell to her father's home. And so it is that when she hears the pitter-patter of little sister's feet coming to greet her she can't help but smile knowing that after today those feet will never pitter-patter quite the same way again.

HER DOLLHOUSE IS YELLOW WITH

blue shutters. She got the dollhouse for her sixth birthday, which was a little over two months ago. So far little sister and daddy have wired it for electricity, papered the walls, carpeted the bedrooms, and painted the exterior.

This weekend is all about the kitchen. They are gluing a white ceramic tile to the floor; tonight they will grout, tomorrow install the kitchen cabinets.

Little sister points. The cabinets are lined up on her dresser. With them, a miniature refrigerator, a stove, a table with chairs, and a sink.

"Did you have a dollhouse when you were little?" Laney's sister has almond-shaped eyes, a blonde bob.

Their father answers, "She sure did."

"What color, Daddy?"

"Yellow with blue shutters."

Laney looks at her father; funny what we choose to recreate.

"I sure did. May I?"

Daisy nods.

Laney collects the wooden family members. One by one she brings them into the living room, seats them on the couch. The mother in her checkered apron, the father, daughter between them, baby in bassinet. "I like it better when everyone's in the same room."

Little sister is next to her now. "Me too."

So close Laney feels the girl's breath touch her ear. Laney

could, if she wanted to, turn her head and spit on the innocent thing. Or she can do what she does, take her little sister into her lap, cuddle her.

Barbara, back from her morning bike ride calls them to the table. She is a pleasant enough woman. Slightly worn but shiny.

"My goodness, Laney, you look so much like your father." This is the third time, "Can you believe it, Rodge? She has your face shape, look at the angle of her jaw and her eyes—"

If Laney had been given up for adoption—matching features might be interesting.

"You are just breathtaking, Laney."

But she's spent years doing this, searching through old photographs, collecting clues. "Can't really take any credit for that."

It amazes Laney. People just don't get it. Appearance is arbitrary. And if it's not arbitrary then it's compensation. Pretty face, ugly heart. Either way it's not something earned, not something she's entitled to say thank you for.

"No surprise to me. Her mother's beautiful." Roger bites into his sandwich.

Laney, habitually polite, lifts a forkful of chicken salad to her mouth and smiles.

There is fruit for dessert, a bit more conversation, and now it's time to leave. "I have to grab my bag."

Laney hurries into Daisy's room. She takes it in: the canopy bed, the collection of teddy bears, the dollhouse. Laney kneels; they look so nice, the little wooden family sitting there like that. She runs her finger across each of their heads. Then she takes the father and drops him in her bag.

Barbara is waiting in the foyer. Daisy next to her. Dad's out front in the car.

"Don't be a stranger," Barbara says.

Laney nods, tucks a strand of shiny blonde hair behind her sister's ear, and continues out the door.

The ride back to the hotel is quiet. There is nothing and everything to say. Laney is looking out the window when Roger starts. "I was eight years old when I hit my first home run. I was so excited I ran all the way home from school. Completely out of my mind—*pop*—brought in three runs."

Roger slows for the light. "I still remember the pitcher's name: Joe Finelli, Italian kid. Anyway, I took the stairs two at a time. 'Ma,' I shouted, 'Ma!' I couldn't wait to tell her. I didn't even knock; I just pushed open her bedroom door. And there she was, unconscious, face-down on the floor, a small pool of vomit around her mouth."

Laney's confused, "I thought she had cancer."

"Nah. Drank herself to death." Roger looks at his daughter, "Your mother and I came up with cancer. How do you explain suicide to a kid? Anyway, it took me until I was fifty years old to not be angry."

Something about the way Roger communicates this, his tone, the way he rests his hand on Laney's seat, the concern in his eyes, gives it away.

"Who told you?"

"Your brother called. Rehab wanted family history."

Laney takes a minute, processes.

"I'm not angry, Dad."

"Of course you are."

She is too old, she knows now, it is suddenly too late to pretend. Laney feels for the wooden father in her bag. She should give him back.

The light turns green. Roger signals, turns right.

"I was thinking, maybe I'll bring the girls up north this spring. I hear they're planning on closing The Plaza, turning it into a mall or something. I better introduce Daisy to Eloise before it's too late."

"That's a great idea."

Laney waits for Roger to pull up to the hotel and come to a complete stop before opening the door. "I'll meet you in the city with the kids. We can go on a carousel ride." Laney smiles his smile.

Her father has tears in his eyes. Shame? Regret? Joy?

"The other day I told Janey the story of Pinky Tinkerbink."

"Really?" He turns his head; he can't even look at her.

But then he does. He turns back. "I never stopped loving you, Laney."

Laney gathers herself, leans forward, kisses his cheek. "I know, Dad."

It is early afternoon by the time Laney reaches the pool, which is, actually, the perfect time to go swimming. "Excuse me," she says to the cabana boy, who is for better or worse, far from being a boy. His hair long, body tan. "Can I get a chaise?"

"No problem. What room you in?"

Laney shows him her room key, signs for her towel, and follows him through a sea of white chairs.

"Where are you from?" Laney asks as he opens her umbrella.

"Minnesota."

That's the accent. "Cold in Minnesota."

"Sure is."

"So which are you? A Dylan, Prince, or Replacements guy?"

Cabana Boy smiles. "Grew up ten minutes from the farm where Dylan wrote 'Tangled Up in Blue.'"

"That's cool." Laney waits for him to spread out her towel.

"Anything else you need, Mrs.—?"

"Call me Laney."

"Anything else you need, Laney?"

How to answer that?

"A Bloody Mary would be great, extra spicy." She rests her

sarong on the side of the chair then waits, her body angled toward the sun, for his return.

Which he does. "Here you go," he says, placing the tray on the table beside her. Laney reaches for the celery stick, bites on it. "You're going to think I'm crazy."

"Crazy?"

"Never mind."

Look at Laney acting all bashful.

"Tell me," he says.

She takes her time signing the check. "People must tell you all the time—how much you look like Jesus."

Cabana Boy laughs. "Like Jesus?"

And from the flicker of the sun on his still-white teeth, Laney knows she has him.

BRUCE SITS IN A CHAIR, ELBOWS ON

top the table, head in hands. He uncovers his eyes slowly, like a boy about to see, for the first time, an unmasked Darth Vader. He looks at Laney standing there. Even now, with all of it, she is everything he ever wanted.

"I fell asleep on the beach."

"It doesn't really matter what you did." Bruce's voice is resigned.

"But that's the truth."

"Nah. That's not the truth." He turns away because he'd rather not see it again, the ease in which she lies.

"So you're accusing me of lying to you?"

"I knew you'd twist it like that. Next you'll give me your whole I-don't-understand-your-pain rap."

In the distance, resolute palm trees stand erect despite an illuminated moon. There is stillness between husband and wife. This, the last breath uttered before death.

"Honey, this is a misunderstanding or something," Laney sits on the table, her smooth right calf brushes against his face, "All that happened was—"

"You know Sue called me at the office last week all concerned. Said you were stoned at pick-up."

"Sue Friedman wants to fuck you, Bruce. She's been wanting to fuck you for a year."

"That's a cop-out."

"What, you already fuck her then?"

Laney knows, before the venom escapes from her mouth, that it's too much, too harsh.

"I'm sorry," she says, wiping, with her thumb, the small pool of tears settled in the corner of Bruce's eye, "I'm really sorry."

Laney navigates the swollen Florida air. She pushes it aside, to the right and left. As if the whole of the Miami exists behind a curtain she can open and close with leisure.

She checks her watch. He couldn't have been waiting more than an hour. They are on vacation aren't they? He isn't Mr. Innocent. These theatrics aren't about her being late for dinner. They're about one thing. His needing more.

To play golf at the club, wasn't that what their last fight was over? That she never plays golf at the club. Laney takes a cigarette from her pocket, lights it, inhales. Only in it for the burn, she grins as smoke escapes through her top teeth.

She continues.

He's right: "You're absolutely right, Bruce."

And he is right. She shouldn't have done it. Coke combined with the mood stabilizer she's taking could give her a heart attack. Nearly gave her one.

A line or two with Cabana Boy and her heart began to race, *thump*, *thump*, *thump*. She was scared she was dying. Scared to come back to the hotel for help. She didn't want Bruce to get all mad at her, freak out, send her to rehab again or something. So she took some Xanax, too many Xanax, came down and fell asleep. She must be crazy. "I must be crazy."

By now, her saying this is rhetorical. Crazy, not crazy, there's no excuse for her behavior. She isn't so crazy that she doesn't know what she's doing. She knew exactly what she was doing. And she wanted to.

"If you're not mad at me, Bruce, then why are you looking at me like that?"

"I'm just looking at how pretty you are."

In the recess of her mind, Bruce's voice sounds no different than that of a toad. The toad inside Laney's head hops about with the ease and candor of a tenor with laryngitis. *How pretty you are. How pretty you are.*

And then, aware that mirrored images lie, she wonders if it's a question. *Me? Pretty?*

Something about this makes her want to laugh but Laney, eager to claim any gesture on Bruce's part as one of forgiveness, throws her arms around his shoulders and kisses him. "You're the pretty one, Bruce."

The warts, Laney supposes, the warts on a toad's chin move in synchronicity with his mouth.

Memory, relentless, travels in and out of her head. She looks beyond her bedroom window; to the star she is being told to wish on. "Close your eyes and make a wish, sweetheart."

Laney solicits, without much thought, the apple-green Schwinn she saw in the window of the bike store. She doesn't think to ask for quiet. Doesn't think to ask, "Why?" *Why the fuck should I wish on a star, Ma?*

She looks up. Clouds, even obscured by a fading light, mutate from turtle to rabbit to ghost. It was a game. Dad driving, Mom in the passenger seat. She and Roost are in the back. They are on their way to the beach.

Laney is pointing through the sunroof, insisting that the cloud, the one straight ahead, at twelve o'clock, is a turtle. Her brother spots an elephant, her mom a dog with a C-shaped tail.

The sound of what was, the crunch of potato chips, sports radio, heavy trucks rattling by, grip Laney like a vise. *An arrangement could not be made between Jackson and the Yankees.*

It's all up to Bruce, how much he's willing to forgive. But why, why would he forgive her again?

No, she instructs herself, "No!"

Laney decides here and now that she will surrender the burden of why to those that frequent opera, write television commercials, movies. Why did Bruce put up with her? Why is he really looking at her like this? Why? The why of it, must be limited to the after—when there's time for it, for why.

If she were smart, Laney would leave it here on the hotel balcony. The two of them waiting for the moon to rise. But she can't help herself. "Really though, why are you looking at me like that, Bruce?"

He takes a moment. "I love you so much," he says. Again with tears in his eyes.

And with this Laney's certain. Not today, or even tomorrow. But it will happen. Eventually he'll give up and move on.

"I love you," the toad croaks. I love you, the guilty man's alibi.

IF THE CASTLE IS HOPE, MEMORY IS

the moat that surrounds it. Complete and all consuming, it swallows its traveler whole. "Deliver me," Laney slurs to the silent fear that contains her. She is, no longer, special.

Relegated, all five-foot-six of her, to one of the begging masses. It is here that she finds herself. And all Bruce can think to say is, "Will you ever be at peace, Laney?"

Bruce stands above her waiting for an answer. Jeans and a pale blue t-shirt. It is another morning. Another day in this life.

Laney wants to hate him for remembering her promise. But she can't. She can only turn away. "I don't know, Bruce," she says staring at half-packed luggage.

It isn't him as much as them. Their tiny fists marking every occasion. Crumbled cookies and Applejacks. Laney resents her children for making her feel this way. Making her feel so scared. Sad and responsible. Trapped.

Stuck somewhere between unable and unwilling she refuses to exist in the now. She chooses, instead, to relish the glory of what was. And wasn't. Laney, in love with the idea of tragedy— an ailing father—his last breath a plea for forgiveness.

But Dad didn't die. In fact, he's thriving. Another second-chance father, little-league coach, carpooler. How she hates him, still, for surviving.

Laney tears at it, memory. The command each time was

"Smile" and she obeyed. This showing of teeth—a singular weapon in her battle to evade the ensuing flash of light. The photograph, ablaze in her mind, mutates. She is, at once, bride, mother, and child.

All images fade to black and she's here again. Stark naked against the white of day. To what end, Laney wonders, does each new kiss serve, only to reaffirm. Solemn was the gentle touch of Janey's damp eyelashes as they pressed against her cheek. "Just two days," Laney assured. "Two days and Mommy and Daddy will be home."

It wasn't entirely her fault this time. Standing at the edge of her driveway, waving at a departing school bus, Laney was stung by the quick right hook of pavement. She felt off balance and confused. She was, again, at the precipice of the drawbridge. Solitary.

Far from shore, on a wave runner with Cabana Boy, Laney began to feel better.

Speed. Sun. Ocean.

She fucked him for the magic, for whatever it was that made her feel whole. She promised she wouldn't do that anymore, fuck to confirm.

Faith.

Confounded by the notion of appointed salvation—isn't religion a salve for the ignorant that build the churches—it is easier for Laney to swallow. How to convey this to her expectant husband. That some days are just too difficult.

Every gesture a nod to the absurd. To live, to continue, to believe. Love, any and all, works only to underscore the inevitable. Death lingers, all consuming.

A diaper change—the gentle removal of waste from her baby's ass—Laney won't get to take that with her. No, in death she will take nothing. And therein lies the rub—to be happy *in spite of.*

"Maybe I shouldn't care anymore." Bruce's tone is flat. She has, finally, exhausted him.

Relief washes over Laney's, as yet, unbaptised face. "Maybe," she answers without moving her eyes from their luggage, "Maybe, you shouldn't."

It is with this that Laney rises to select her shoes. Which to wear: sneakers, heels, beaded thongs? She decides, after much deliberation, on a pair of navy running shoes.

"YOU'RE KILLING ME," BRUCE SAYS.

Midday flight.

"You know that, right? That you're killing me?"

Laney doesn't answer. She chooses, instead, to pass her husband the foiled half of the York Peppermint Patty she bought at the newsstand just before boarding. After restraining himself for at least twenty seconds, he says quietly, but loud enough for Laney to hear, "York Peppermint Patty. Get the sensation."

Through the oval-shaped passenger window Laney can see the flight's luggage being carted, with indifference, from terminal to plane. She addresses Bruce without looking at him, "What's the sensation?"

"The sensation?"

She turns. "You just said, 'York Peppermint Patty. Get the sensation.' What do you think the sensation is?" This a peace offering on her part. An acknowledgement.

Bruce crumbles the wrapper, places it in the seat pocket in front of him. "When did you start hating me, Lane?"

Laney returns her attention to the baggage. She'd pay them if she could, those men out there, pay them to kick her suitcase off that truck. To start over. A few t-shirts, couple pair of jeans, a knapsack. But even at birth, she grins, the obvious play on words, "You're born with baggage."

"What about baggage?"

She looks at him, without hiding. "I don't hate you, Bruce."

Bruce runs his fingers through his hair, clasps his hands.

"What is it then? Because you know, I try so hard, Lane. Everything I do is for you and the kids."

She knows this is true. That they are, that she is, loved by him.

"It has nothing to do with you."

"What's it have to do with then?"

"I'm not sure."

"Is it that you're unhappy?"

"No, that's not it exactly. It's not that I'm unhappy—I'm just not happy like I thought I'd be."

Even amid minty-fresh air, the stench of Bruce's disdain is palpable. "I'll tell you what's wrong with you, Laney." He leans in her direction, "You're a spoiled fucking cunt."

Laney's response is to shush him. She does this by bringing her finger to her mouth.

"You care what these people think?" He points in the direction of passengers.

She pulls his arm down. "We're going to be kicked off the plane."

"Terrific."

Nothing is said for quite some time. A minute, maybe longer.

"You never cease to amaze me, Laney. Here you are worried about getting kicked off the plane for inappropriate behavior, yet you don't seem to give two shits—"

Laney's about to speak but Bruce shuts her down. "I guess that's part of it, though. You'd probably feel better if I did that, right? If I kicked you out of the house. You'd probably feel some warped sense of validation. Like you were right after all: all men, not just your father, all men are assholes."

Bruce takes a breath. "Well you're never going to be that lucky because for some reason, Lane," his voice cracks. "For some reason, no matter how many times you disappoint me, I can't stop loving you."

Everything Bruce just said is true. She is a spoiled fucking cunt who wants to be kicked out of her house so she can blame him for the second half of her failed life. She is all that and a coward. A coward. A druggie. A hurtful person to be around.

Laney reaches for Bruce's shoulders and is able to pull, without opposition, his lunk of a head to her chest. Bruce laughs as he sniffles through tears, "And they say you're the fucked-up one."

There is a movie on board and they watch it. Wet eggs are delivered and pushed away. Coffee. They drink the coffee. It's an easy flight. Smooth landing.

And at baggage claim, as if to taunt, no, more to reaffirm, to underscore—At baggage claim, as if to underscore what Laney is already well aware of, hers is the first piece of luggage dropped onto the carousel.

Simple are the letters. Four.

H.

The chauffer-driven town car turns into their driveway.

Pumpkins, eager to be carved, flank the front door. In a few days Laney will, as promised, turn them into jack-o-lanterns. Illumination a pledge. This, theirs, a warm home filled with candy.

O.

Laney checks the time, 3:15 p.m., then calculates. Seventeen hours? Is that right? She can do it, keep herself together for— no it's eighteen hours. Ten of which are sleep. Eli's piano recital, dinner, bath, sleep.

Tomorrow. 8 a.m. Tomorrow at 8 a.m. she'll tell Dr. Page everything that happened, dig into her bag, bring out the wooden doll. Maybe he'll suggest an additional day of therapy, recommend a different medication. Whatever the specifics, Laney will continue, for as long as she possibly can, to play out her role in this drama.

M.

The sedan pulls to a stop. Out step a man and a woman. A man and his wife. The stunned silence between them cut by the reverberation of laughter. The front door, shiny and red, opens. Through it run two children, a boy and a girl. They are shouting, "Mommy." "Daddy." "Mommy." "Daddy." The woman kneels down, scoops the little girl into her arms. The man lifts the boy in the air.

E.

MRS. MATTINGLY, PIANO TEACHER

and future member of the Woodcliff parent body, hosts seasonal recitals in the living room of her home. The fall recital, traditionally given the Sunday before Thanksgiving break, is taking place a month early this year due to the impending birth of Mrs. Mattingly's first child, a girl.

Janey Brooks, carpool companion come de facto student, as well as mother to eight baby dolls herself, has maintained an interest, bordering on obsession, in Mrs. Mattingly's growing belly. Mrs. Mattingly, aware of the effect a pregnant belly can have on a little girl, has been kind enough to include Janey in the fun. The four-year-old has evaluated sonogram pictures, been consulted on shades of pink paint color, and has even, on not one but two occasions, weighed in on possible baby names.

So it is that Miss Jane Raleigh Brooks, although not a participant in today's recital, enters Mrs. Mattingly's living room in her finest regalia: Smock dress. Patent leather shoes. Purse.

Her brother, on the other hand, not one for piano recitals, babies, or the Izod and khaki pant ensemble his mother laid out on the bed for him, is sporting a Knicks jersey and gym shorts. Shorts that are so long he may just as well be wearing sweats.

Seated now, in the fourth of six rows of foldout chairs rented for the occasion, the Brooks family, at first glance, look like any other family. Bruce, arm over son's shoulder, holds the recital program in his free hand. Janey is admiring her pretty pink shoes.

Laney's busy chatting to another mother, "Next Thursday's fine…"

Now zoom in.

Notice the small lines around Laney's mouth, the taught jaw. Observe the way she's playing with the ends of her hair. Note her defensive, hurried tone. Laney, aisle seat, back to family, waves as friends approach—jumps to kiss—cheek, cheek—even lunges into the aisle at times. Anything necessary to block them from seeing—Laney turns to check. Eli looks at ease, maybe he's getting better, certainly the intervals between eye contortions are fewer and farther apart.

Or are they?

And now there's this new thing he does with his mouth. Eli repeats the ritual. He twists his mouth, holds his lips in a tight squeeze, waits a beat, releases. Laney can't stand it—"You look like you're sucking on a lemon," she wants to say but doesn't. Instead she stands at attention, ready to bite.

Only after Mrs. Mattingly signals it's time to begin, "Welcome everybody," does Laney let her guard down and allow herself to sit.

"Today's performances," Mrs. Mattingly continues, "are organized by age, youngest to oldest respectively. Each student…" Laney begins calculating. Eight performances at, what, ten minutes each? She checks the time—back by six. That's do-able.

A mother of a student, the same mother that brought Mrs. Mattingly the gorgeous flower arrangement that adorns the piano, is asking something.

"What's that, Alison?"

Alison tries again, "I said aren't you going to play for us?"

Mrs. Mattingly smiles, "—Well…" A mild chanting. "Mrs. Mattingly. Mrs. Mattingly…"

"If it will get you to stay for the pizza."

Janey looks to her mother as if to say, "Can we?" To which

Laney nods her head yes even though she has no intention of keeping on here through dinner.

It's not the menu that's making Laney anxious. There are all sorts of ways to manage pizza. It's not the fact that Eli's ticking away like a madman either. If anyone happens to notice they'll think that's the way he chews his food.

Laney surveys the room. Bankers, money managers, physicians. Moms, Dads, Stepparents, Grandparents, Caregivers, Housekeepers, Nannies. At first, the best of them will be quite awed—the pregnant lady's fingers dancing across the keyboard. Some may feel genuine admiration. The precision, the discipline it must take—So engrossed they dare not bring the cheesy slice to their lips—Imagine, to have mastered…

Soon though their minds will drift to the dinner party they're planning, the business meeting tomorrow, the bridge game. And that's when the esteem, that only minutes before inspired, will begin to mutate into a reflexive disgust. Pizza in. All that practice. Bite. Hours upon hours to end up a piano teacher.

Happiness, Laney's sure, is somehow related to the rapidity in which one is able to implement denial. *Want to learn to play the piano? Please, I'm too busy working on my handicap.*

Laney leans in close, speaks softly, "I hate this."

"What?" There is no accusation in Bruce's tone. He's trying to be nice. Last night, his voice communicates, is in the past—almost. How amazing it must be, to have his ability to compartmentalize and move on.

"All these chin-up, hands-folded, closed-lipped, self-satisfied phonies. Acting like they give a shit about this piano recital."

"I give a shit."

Laney smiles. She's going to be friendly too. "Okay, you give a shit. And I'm sure there are a couple others. But mostly everyone's here to cover themselves. It's the 'right thing' to do. Good parents go to piano recitals, great parents remember to bring the teacher flowers."

"But not you."

"I'm honest at least. I'm not going to put my head down tonight and feel better about myself because I came to this."

Bruce doesn't say anything.

"That woman asked Mrs. Mattingly to play the piano because she wants everyone in the room to know that she cares. Not only about her kid—but she cares about Mrs. Mattingly."

"What's bad about that?"

"Because it's all about her, don't you see? It's about maintaining a perception. Despite the diamond watch, she's a woman with compassion."

In an effort to show he hasn't completely dismissed her theory, Bruce points to Drew Heskel, a widower. Drew, an entertainment attorney with twins in second grade is sitting up front, a daughter in each arm. "What's his agenda?"

Drew's agenda's easy. This is an opportunity to show his dead wife's friends that he's a good guy despite his dating the twins' twenty-four-year-old babysitter. Drew Heskel takes Mrs. Mattingly aside after her performance. Volunteers to help her copyright her composition: "Vanishing," a symphony for children.

Offers access to free studio time. Even has the gumption to say to Mrs. Mattingly's architect husband, Bill—as if by marrying and building a family with her, he hadn't demonstrated conviction—"She's just too good not to be a star."

To which Bill concurs and Mrs. Mattingly, Joyce, blushes, "You're kind but—" She touches her swollen belly, "This is enough blessing."

Later in the evening though, Laney's certain. After the napkins are picked up off the floor, the chairs folded, the pizza boxes stacked and tied, Joyce Mattingly, belly protruding from not-too-warm-it-might-hurt-the-fetus bath water, will wonder, smile to herself even at the mere possibility.

Bruce isn't capable of understanding how it's a crime really.

To offer hope when there is none. But before Laney can even try to explain this, she is interrupted by applause. Jill Shields has finished and is taking a bow.

"You're next, buddy." Bruce pats their son on the back.

Mrs. Mattingly begins, "As most of you know, Beethoven was completely without hearing by the time he wrote the Ninth Symphony."

There is murmuring in the room.

"I know. I can't process it myself."

She waits for the audience to quiet.

"Much of course, has been written about Beethoven having been deaf, but my favorite story is this. After the first performance of the Ninth, Beethoven stared blankly at his orchestra. A thoughtful musician, realizing Beethoven couldn't hear the clapping, turned the conductor around to face the audience. It was his eyes, not his ears, that conveyed the symphony's triumph.

"And now without further ado I'd like to introduce Eli Brooks. Eli will be performing the final movement of the Ninth, The Ode to Joy." Mrs. Mattingly smiles in Eli's direction, beckoning. The boy, all of three-foot-seven, stands, proceeds down the aisle, one foot in front of the other. He pulls back the piano bench, fixes his music.

And then amazingly, without any twitching of the neck, contorting of the mouth, blinking of the eyes, begins to play— fingers on keys, wrists raised.

This, the sound of her son, is, perhaps, the most beautiful Laney's ever heard. Again she is reminded that she is too old, that it is too late for her to pretend she is anything other than what she is.

But she is—at least for this moment—okay with that.

NAKED, BATH FILLING WITH BUBBLES,

Laney hurries into her closet. She grabs the stool, takes a step, and reaches for a shoebox on the top shelf. She pulls it down. Deep in the toe of a pair of black sling backs is a small wax envelope of cocaine.

Laney hurries back to the bathroom. She kneels on the marble floor. Opens the envelope. The powder is white. Unlike bread, cocaine doesn't mold. Or get you fat. Or make you tired.

Laney is thinking about this as she empties the envelope's contents—the good that comes with drugs. No one ever talks about the good.

She cuts the powder with her pinky, sucks the residue off her thumb. It's not as much as she'd like, but it's enough to get her going.

There is a mirror on the bathroom door. Laney glances at her reflection, her legs bent as they are, look like a "greater than" sign. The toilet bowl is greater than—she follows her reflection. Stomach to ribs. Ribs to breast. Breast to neck. Chin to mouth to nose. She stops at her eyes. And then, as if to acknowledge this other presence smiling at her, she smiles back.

So when it happens, when Laney hears whatever it is shatter, she doesn't brush the powder aside and hurry into the kitchen. Instead she presses her cheek against the cool Carrera marble and breathes in through her nose.

"Ma."

Janey is calling her name.

"Laney!" *Fucking Bruce shouting like that.*

Laney licks what remains off the bathroom floor. Like she possesses some God-given talent for cleaning up spilled milk. But it's too late. As she reaches for her bathrobe, the door opens. Eli enters first, followed by Janey.

"I lost my contact." Laney says, tightening the terrycloth belt. She kneels, runs her fingers across the floor, "Damn this thing is hard to find."

They don't respond.

She looks up a second time. Bruce has joined them. He stares at her, doesn't communicate a set agenda, just stares. And then, like any good father would, he takes each child by the shoulder and leads them out the room.

Laney pushes the door closed with the palm of her hand. It is only now that she sees the blood dripping from her nostrils.

And yet again, she meets her eyes in the mirror. And yet again, she smiles.

"I'M GLAD YOU CALLED ME."

Directly behind Donny is a mock up of the spring ad campaign. A life-sized poster, a caricature of Donny's father, sitting on top a cow. Arms in the air, cowboy hat, two lassoed yogurt pops. "The Dairy King Rides Again."

Laney is too wired to sit still. "I need something to calm me down."

"I can't give you anything, Lane. If I did, what kind of person would that make me?"

"Please, Donny. Now isn't the time for moralizing." Laney, still holding a tissue to her nose, smiles.

"But you were just away in—"

"Pleeeease." Her voice childlike for effect.

Donny's cell is ringing, but he ignores it. Instead he wets his thumb, wipes the dry blood from Laney's nose, tucks a piece of Laney's hair behind her ear. "It's all going to be okay," he says.

"No it's not. You're about to have another baby."

"We'll figure it out." Donny kisses Laney's neck, then her mouth.

Now his office phone is ringing. "I better get that." Donny walks over to his desk, opens a drawer, tosses Laney a silver pill case with an enamel unicorn on the cover.

"Hello?"

Laney tries to make out who it is on the other side of the line but can't.

"I'll be right there. Don't worry, everything is going to be okay."

How many people you going to 'make everything okay' for, Donny?

Laney opens the pill case. *Nice.*

"I have to go, Lane. Sorry." He grabs his jacket. "Adam has 104 fever, threw up three times. They're bringing him to the hospital."

"That's terrible."

"Wait for me, okay? I'll be back in a couple hours."

Laney nods her head, lie for lie.

The parking lot is dark. In the bar across the street from Donny's office a neon sign flashes: EVERY NIGHT EIGHTIES NIGHT.

Inside, two fairly worn-out looking blondes are singing a Bon Jovi song on the karaoke machine. *"No one heard a single word she said. They should have seen it in your eyes…"* Laney takes a seat at the bar, orders a beer and begins singing along with them. Quietly and to herself. *"Ooh, she's a little runaway…"*

"You know," the guy at the next stool says, "Roy Bitten from the East Street Band played piano on this track."

"Really." Laney lifts the bottle to her mouth.

"Everyone thinks of Bon Jovi as heavy metal. But Jon wanted to be rock-and-roll, wanted to be Springsteen."

Talker's sporting a cap that says Quaker State Motor Oil. Probably a plumber or an electrician, a man with a trade. He's got a gold watch on his right hand, the sad kind with the stretchy gold band. The kind that's passed down from one generation to the next, the treasured family heirloom that over time exposes itself as silver-plated.

"We all want to be something bigger than we are I guess."

"Yeah?" he says, moving closer. "What did you want to be?"

"Me?" Laney tries to make out the tattoo on his arm.

"You see me talking to anyone else?" He has a roughness

to him that reminds Laney of the young Bruce. T-tops down,
stereo blasting.

"All I ever wanted was to get married and live happily ever
after."

"And?"

Laney pulls back, "And what?"

Having hit a speedbump, the tradesman decides to come at it
from a different angle.

"So, what's a nice girl like you doing in a place like this?"

Laney, just to amuse herself, waits a beat. "Who said I'm a
nice girl?"

IT IS AS IF SHE CAN TASTE IT NOW,

almost. Closer. Laney is getting closer.

See the smoke in the distance. She runs toward it only to stop.

"Stop!" The guy from the bar is addressing shoulder blades. Laney's cheek pressed up against brick. She is aware that it could scratch, will most likely.

A pulsing car alarm pleads to a deaf ear. Lights flicker through still-open windows. Well-lit dining rooms are warm. Laney could scream. If she wanted to. She could scream along with the car alarm.

It should only be a minute, maybe two. A minute or two, a whimper, a release. The bugs. The bugs will return. Or is it a rainbow? Which was it last time? A rainbow? Rainbow bugs? Tragedy. Tragedy is multi-hued.

Dry wave. Wet heat. Lie. Liar. Consumes. Consume. It is everyness—wreckage. This wall. The everyness of this brick wall. More stoic than an oak it blinds itself. Why doesn't he have to smell it? The piss on this wall.

"Smell it." Laney says this, doesn't mean to.

"Smell what, baby?"

"Smell my ass hairs," she answers without turning, perhaps without speaking. It is utterly indistinguishable. The real from the absolute.

"Your ass hairs, baby? I'll tell you how your ass hairs smell."

Is that what he's doing now? "Are you licking my ass?"

There is no one to blame. Daddy will send emails. Bruce forgive. *There are medications... to curb the impulses*—"Ha!"

He pushes harder.

Eyes. All those eyes. Too many flickering sets of eyes. Peering through her. Determining:

What exactly?

Laney wants none of it. No more carving from stone. "No more, fucker."

"I'll tell you when it's no more," he says drawing her head back and slamming it against the brick.

She feels better. An answer: the brick scraped her cheek. As she reaches for the wound he pulls her arm back. "Fuck that hurts."

He likes this. "How bad, baby. How bad does it hurt?"

"It hurts good, baby. Good."

Laney is laughing now. A cool, hard, calculated laugh. She could have done it differently. There are ways. She could have bought shoes. That's what other people like her do. A woman at rehab bought shoes, hid them under her bed. Credit card debt—he's sure pounding the shit out of her—is negotiable.

Laney continues, her laugh purely for effect. Nothing new. A put on. Laugh and the man feels bigger. Or smaller. Laugh and he'll turnaround, face the camera as if to say, "See? See how she's taunting me?"

When he does this, you run. Go. Don't look back. Never. Never look back.

Keep laughing. Laugh until you hit this wall and then ask him, "What's all the excitement, big boy? Your wife don't let you up her ass?"

Smug cement is, forgets it's porous.

Bang.

He broke it, Laney thinks. *Motherfucker broke my cheek.*

When it's over she sinks to the pavement. He snickers watching her descend. It doesn't matter though. In time. In time he too will be exposed for what he is. Wife and kids? Fag?

Draw Curtain. Draw Curtain.

In the movie this, here, would be a dark alley in lower Manhattan. Not behind a dumpster in a suburban strip mall. In the movie, that, the small gap between his two front teeth, would be all that illuminates the space between them.

Or gold.

In the movie the costume designer could choose to go with gold. Make the fucker black. Was it rape? Then bounce light off his single gold tooth.

No, the black man as metaphor is cliché. White—in the movie he'd remain white. White man. White teeth. Almost nothing suggests depravity as well as a set of tidy white teeth.

But this, Laney is aware, is less than a movie, a dream even. It's as if the guy standing there laughing doesn't exist because he doesn't. His face blends with the others, his laugh.

He, like they all do, offers, "Want?"

Laney can't move her lips. The gash on her cheek is throbbing, her jaw.

He throws them at her anyway. Five white pills. She is able to ground each, but one, into the asphalt with the heel of her shoe before her eyes close.

"Bitch."

He is gone. This much Laney's certain of. The ironworker, whoever he was, is gone now.

Sirens.

More sirens.

Closer.

No. Not closer.

Laney tries to stand. Pull herself up off the ground but can't.

The ambulance hurls to a stop. Two men, both in uniform, leap. The younger grabs a stretcher. The older runs toward her.

"What happened?"

"I fell," she says, her lips barely parting.

"Some fall."

She tries to smile, but can't. Can't smile, can't bat her eyes, can't push her chest in his face. She has nothing with which to tempt him. She is too ugly.

Finally. Finally she is ugly.

LANEY'S CHEEK, STITCHED AND COVERED

with tape, doesn't hurt. At least not in the way she would have imagined it might. In fact, the throbbing, which is what it mostly feels like now, is a relief. The scar reveals the truth. Anyone looking at her will know now what she is, who she—

This is what Laney's thinking about as the taxi slows in front of her home. It is early morning but the light in Eli's room is on. She waves and waits.

Here's Mommy.

There is no waving back. Just light. Glowing. Yellow.

You know I'm here, right? Know Mommy loves you?

A squirrel, acorn in mouth, dashes across the front lawn in preparation for yet another winter.

Laney takes it all in, the red door, the black shutters, the pumpkins. It is a pretty house, her house. She had, for a little while at least, nearly had it all.

"We can go now," she says to the driver.

Regret vivid and whole is afterthought.

Brazen.

Also published by *Two Dollar Radio*

CRYSTAL EATERS
A NOVEL BY SHANE JONES

"A powerful narrative that touches on the value of every human life, with a lyrical voice and layers of imagery and epiphany." —*BuzzFeed*

"[Jones is] something of a millennial Richard Brautigan." —*Nylon*

A QUESTIONABLE SHAPE
A NOVEL BY BENNETT SIMS

"[*A Questionable Shape*] is more than just a novel. It is literature. It is life." —*The Millions*

"Presents the yang to the yin of Whitehead's *Zone One*, with chess games, a dinner invitation, and even a romantic excursion."
—*The Daily Beast*

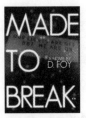

MADE TO BREAK
A NOVEL BY D. FOY

"With influences that range from Jack Kerouac to Tom Waits and a prose that possesses a fast, strange, perennially changing rhythm that's somewhat akin to some of John Coltrane's wildest compositions." —*HTML Giant*

RADIO IRIS
A NOVEL BY ANNE-MARIE KINNEY

"Kinney is a Southern California Camus." —*Los Angeles Magazine*

"[*Radio Iris*] has a dramatic otherworldly payoff that is unexpected and triumphant." —*New York Times Book Review*, Editors' Choice

THE ORANGE EATS CREEPS
A NOVEL BY GRACE KRILANOVICH
* National Book Foundation 2010 '5 Under 35' Selection.
* *NPR* Best Books of 2010.
* *The Believer* Book Award Finalist.

"Krilanovich's work will make you believe that new ways of storytelling are still emerging from the margins." —*NPR*

ANCIENT OCEANS OF CENTRAL KENTUCKY
A NOVEL BY DAVID CONNERLEY NAHM

"Wonderful… Remarkable… it's impossible to stop reading until you've gone through each beautiful line, a beauty that infuses the whole novel, even in its darkest moments." —NPR

HOW TO GET INTO THE TWIN PALMS
A NOVEL BY KAROLINA WACLAWIAK

"One of my favorite books this year." —*The Rumpus*

"Waclawiak's novel reinvents the immigration story."
—*New York Times Book Review*, Editors' Choice

THE PEOPLE WHO WATCHED HER PASS BY
A NOVEL BY SCOTT BRADFIELD

"Challenging [and] original… A billowy adventure of a book. In a book that supplies few answers, Bradfield's lavish eloquence is the presiding constant." —*New York Times Book Review*

"Brave and unforgettable. Scott Bradfield creates a country for the reader to wander through, holding Sal's hand, assuming goodness."
—*Los Angeles Times*

THE CAVE MAN
A NOVEL BY XIAODA XIAO

* *WOSU* (NPR member station) Favorite Book of 2009.

"As a parable of modern China, [*The Cave Man*] is chilling."
—*Boston Globe*

THE DROP EDGE OF YONDER
A NOVEL BY RUDOLPH WURLITZER

* *Time Out New York*'s Best Book of 2008.
* *ForeWord* Magazine 2008 Gold Medal in Literary Fiction.
"A picaresque American *Book of the Dead*… in the tradition of Thomas Pynchon, Joseph Heller, Kurt Vonnegut, and Terry Southern." —*Los Angeles Times*